SHAKE:

MACBETH

RETOLD BY   ILLUSTRATED BY

MARTIN POWELL   F. DANIEL

STONE ARCH BOOKS
a capstone imprint

Retold by Martin Powell
Illustrated by F. Daniel

Series Editor: Sean Tulien
Editorial Director: Michael Dahl
Series Designer: Brann Garvey
Art Director: Bob Lentz
Creative Director: Heather Kindseth

Shakespeare Graphics is published by
Stone Arch Books, 1710 Roe Crest Drive,
North Mankato, Minnesota 56003

WWW.CAPSTONEPUB.COM

Cataloging-in-Publication Data is available
at the Library of Congress website.

ISBN: 978-1-4342-2506-1 (library binding)
ISBN: 978-1-4342-3447-6 (paperback)

Printed and bound in China.
002596

TABLE OF CONTENTS

SHAKESPEARE

WILLIAM SHAKESPEARE WAS ONE OF
THE GREATEST WRITERS THE WORLD
HAS EVER KNOWN.

HE WROTE COMEDIES, TRAGEDIES,
HISTORIES, AND ROMANCES ABOUT
ANCIENT HEROES, BLOODY WARS,
AND MAGICAL CREATURES.

THIS IS ONE OF THOSE STORIES . . .

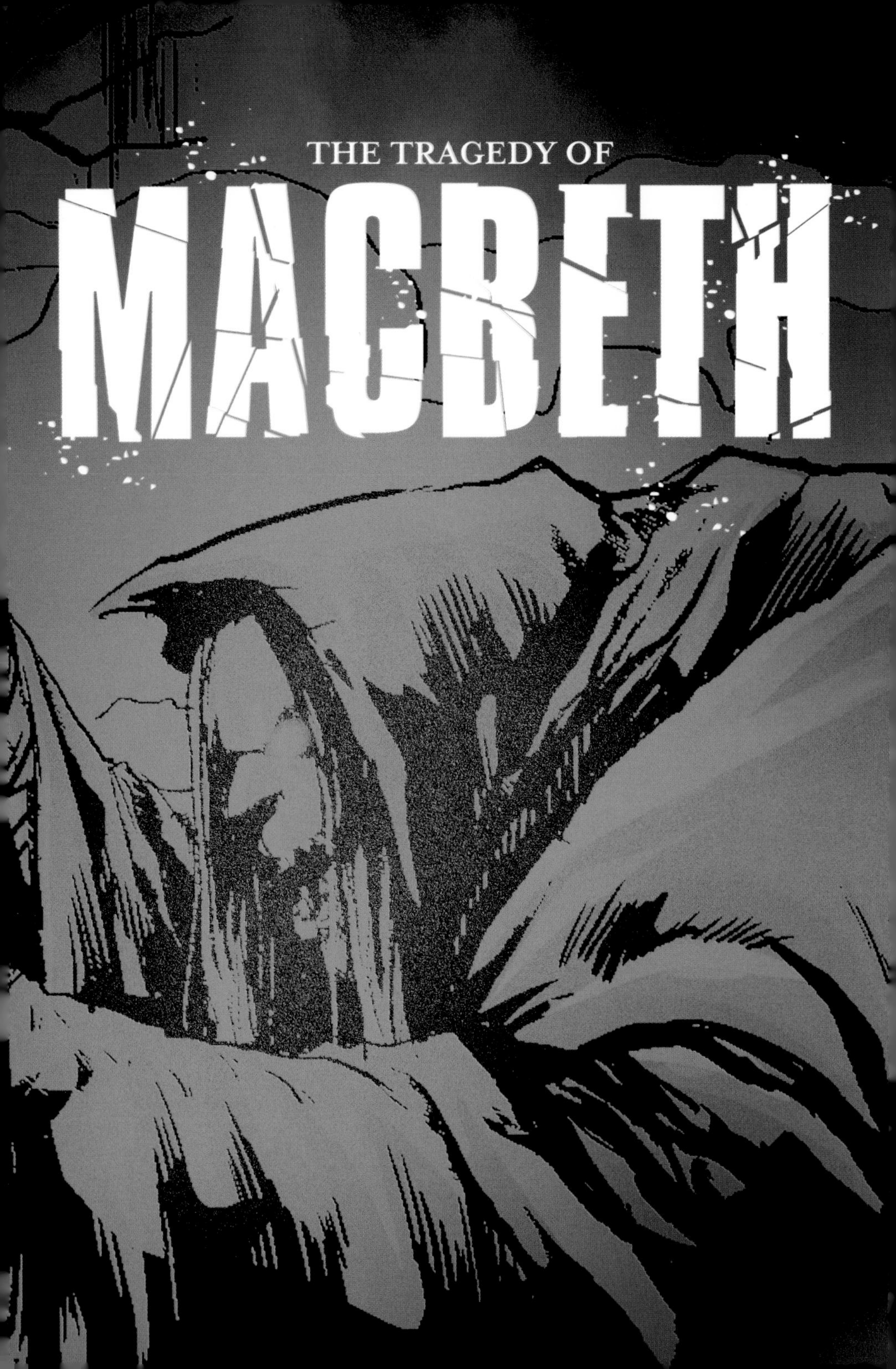
THE TRAGEDY OF
MACBETH

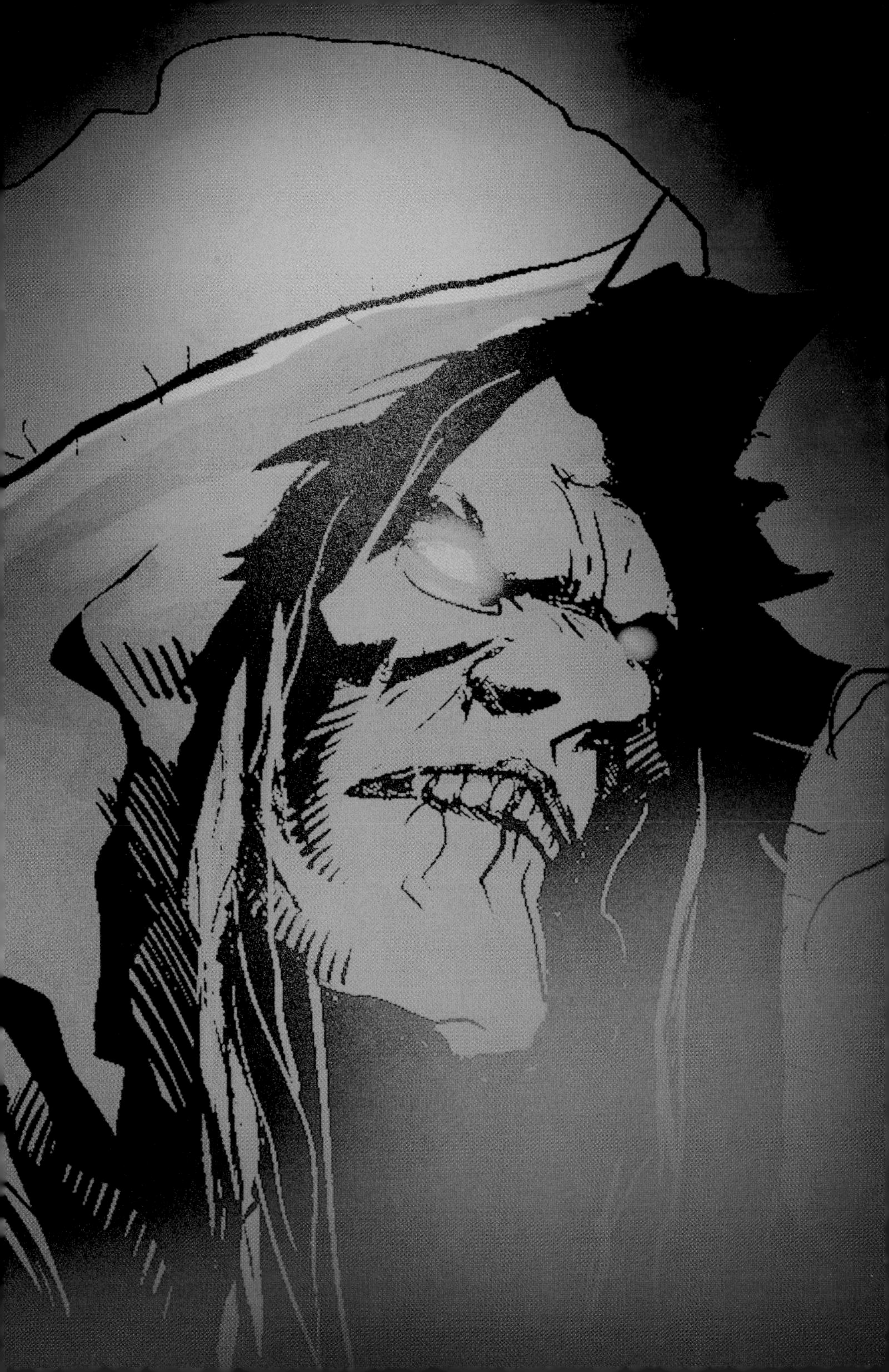

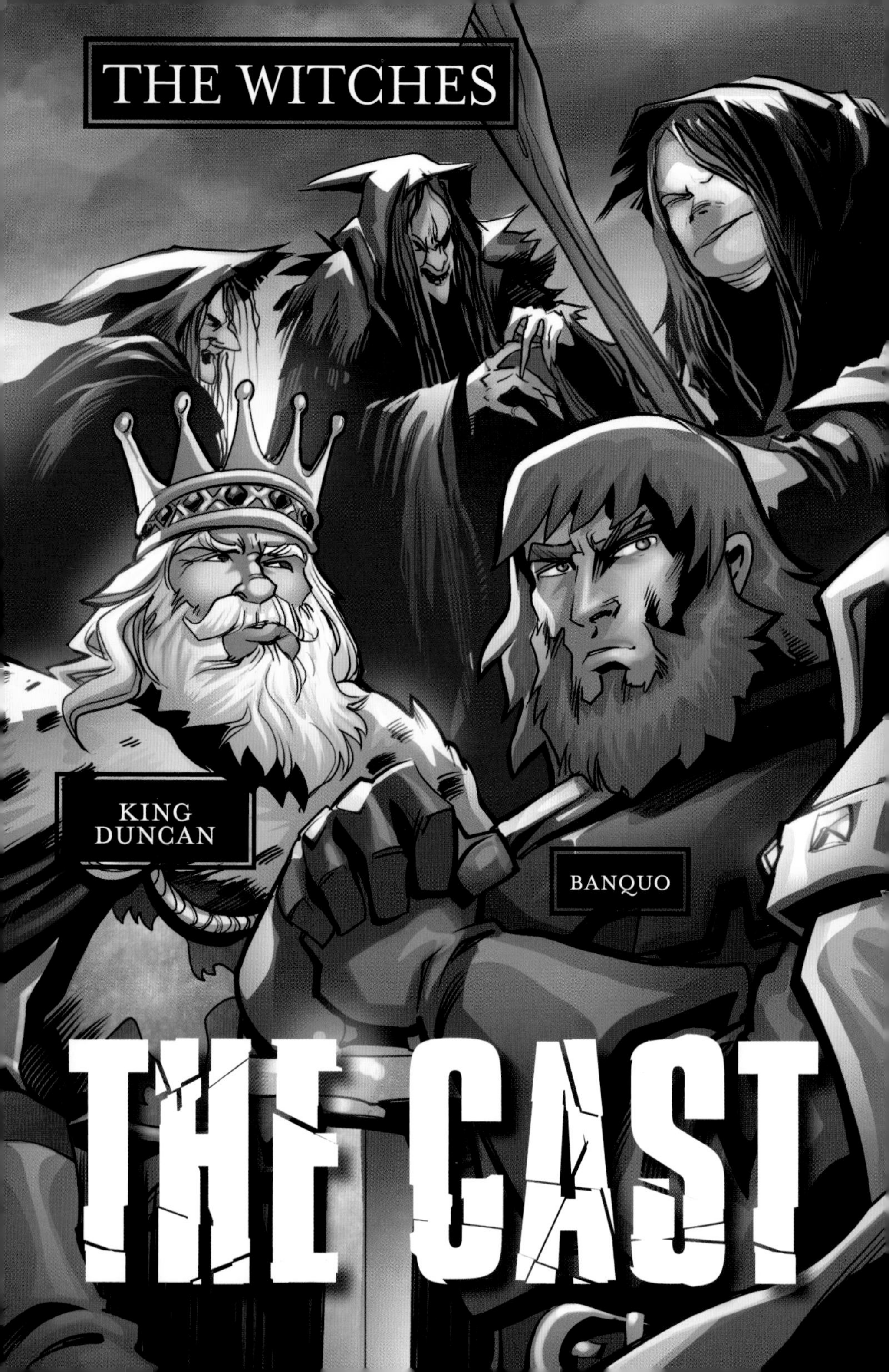
THE WITCHES
KING DUNCAN
BANQUO
THE CAST

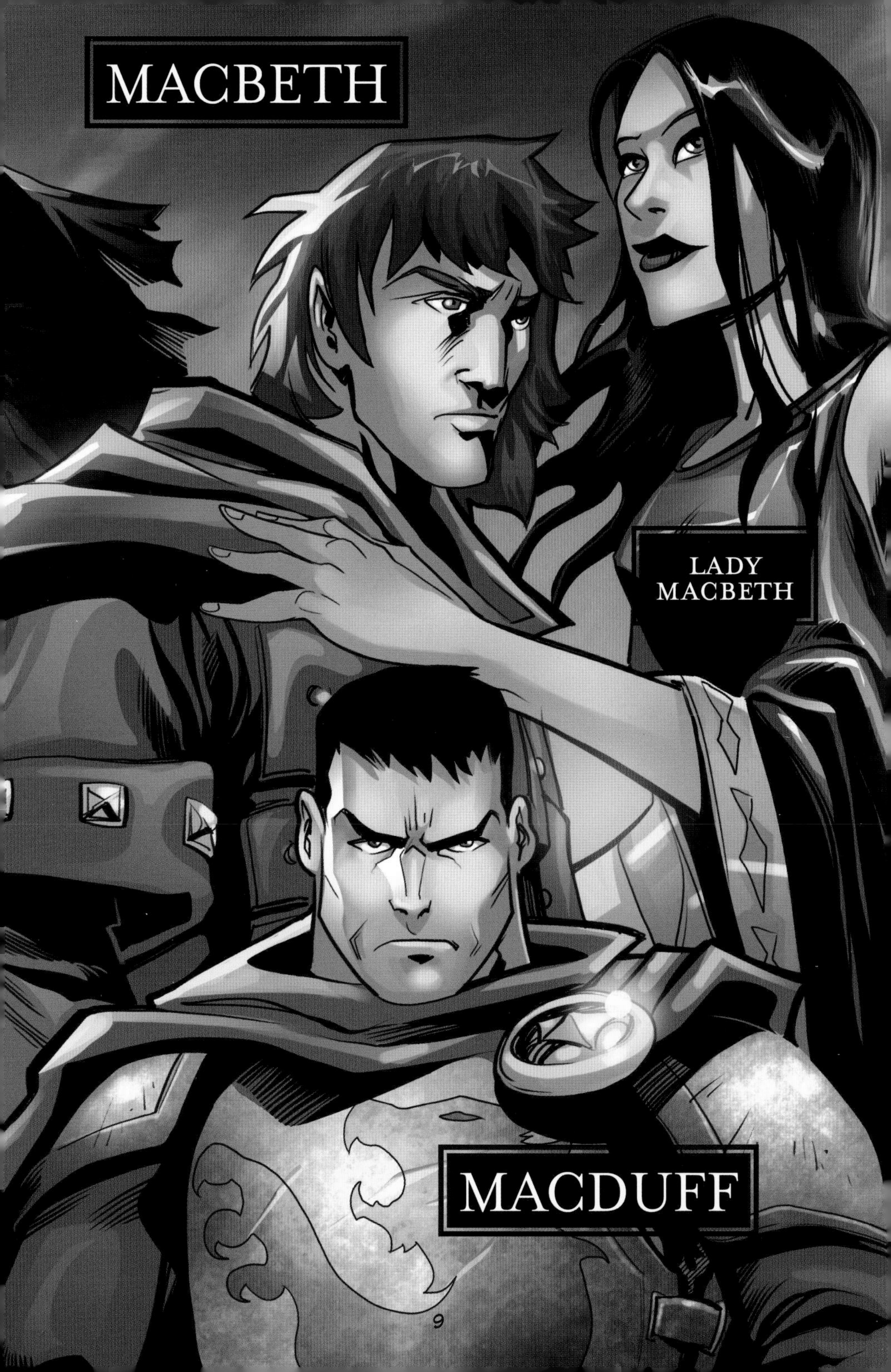
MACBETH
LADY MACBETH
MACDUFF

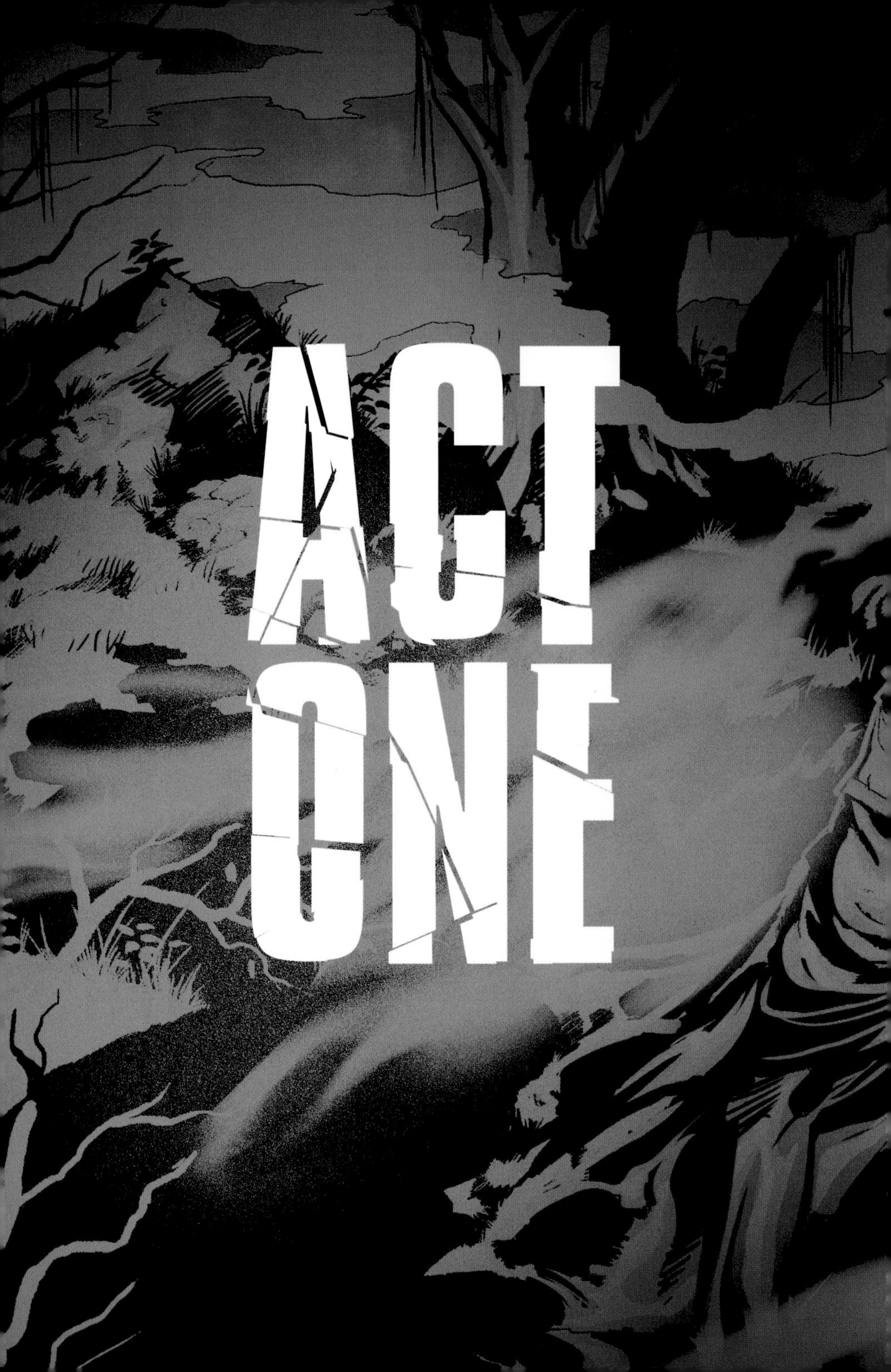

ACT ONE

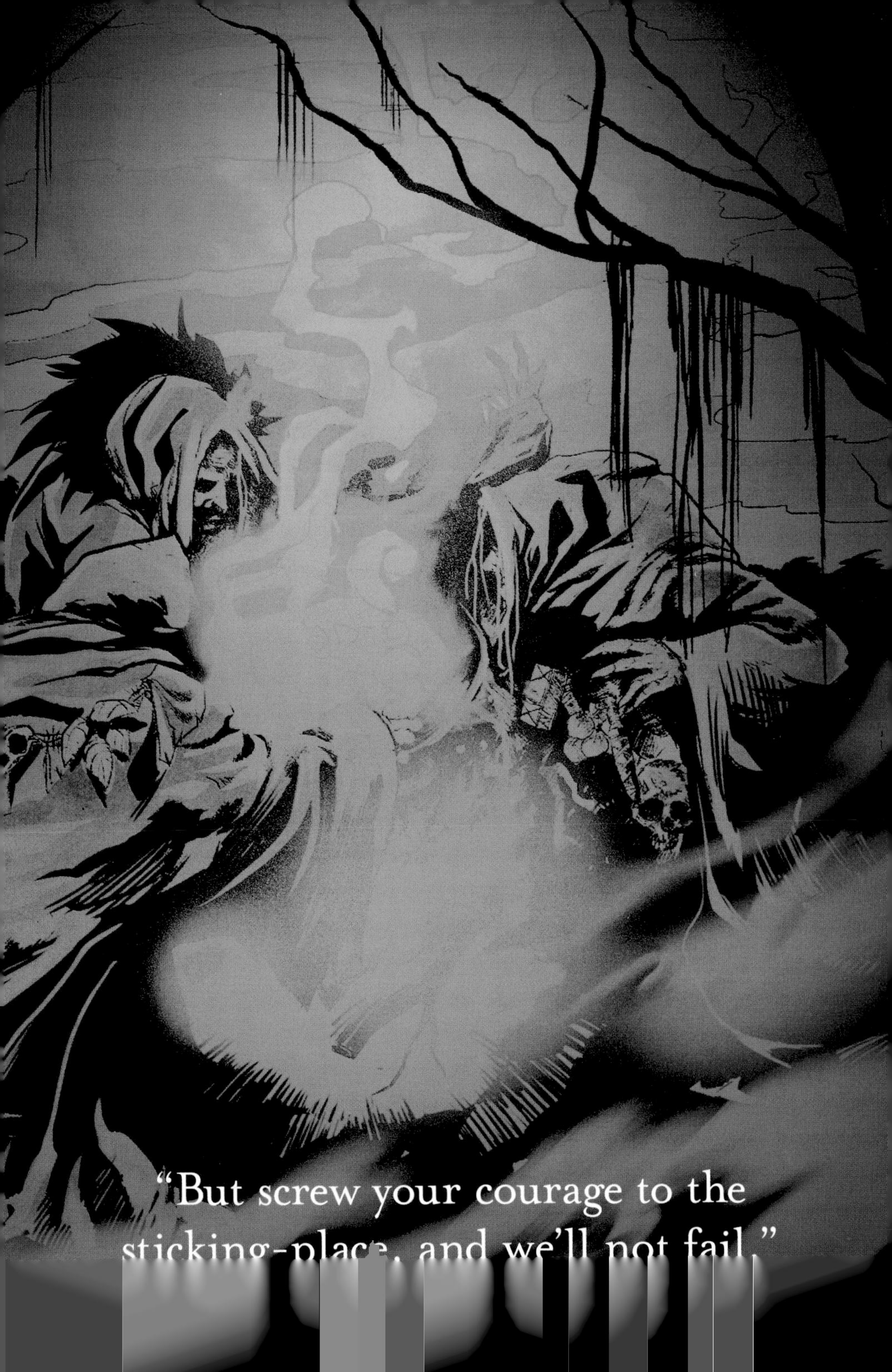
"But screw your courage to the
sticking-place, and we'll not fail."

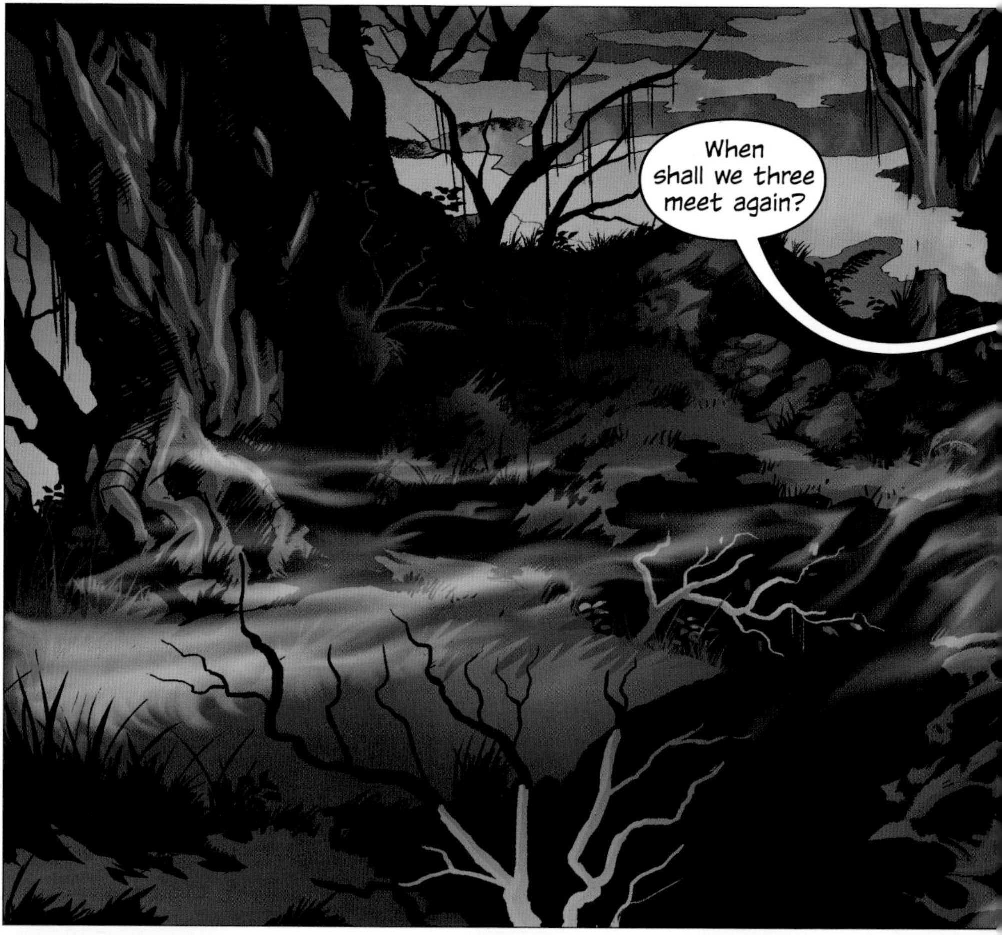
When shall we three meet again?

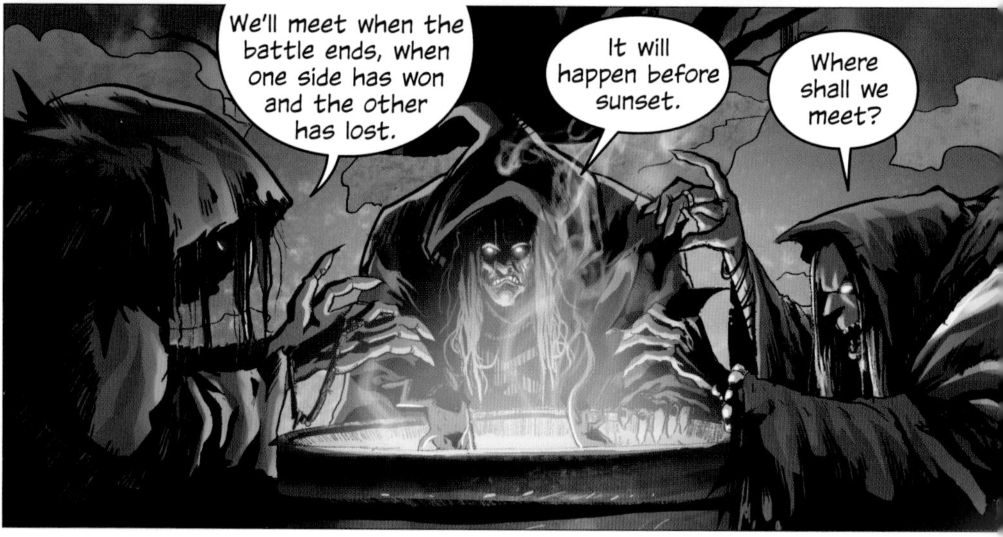
We'll meet when the battle ends, when one side has won and the other has lost.
It will happen before sunset.
Where shall we meet?

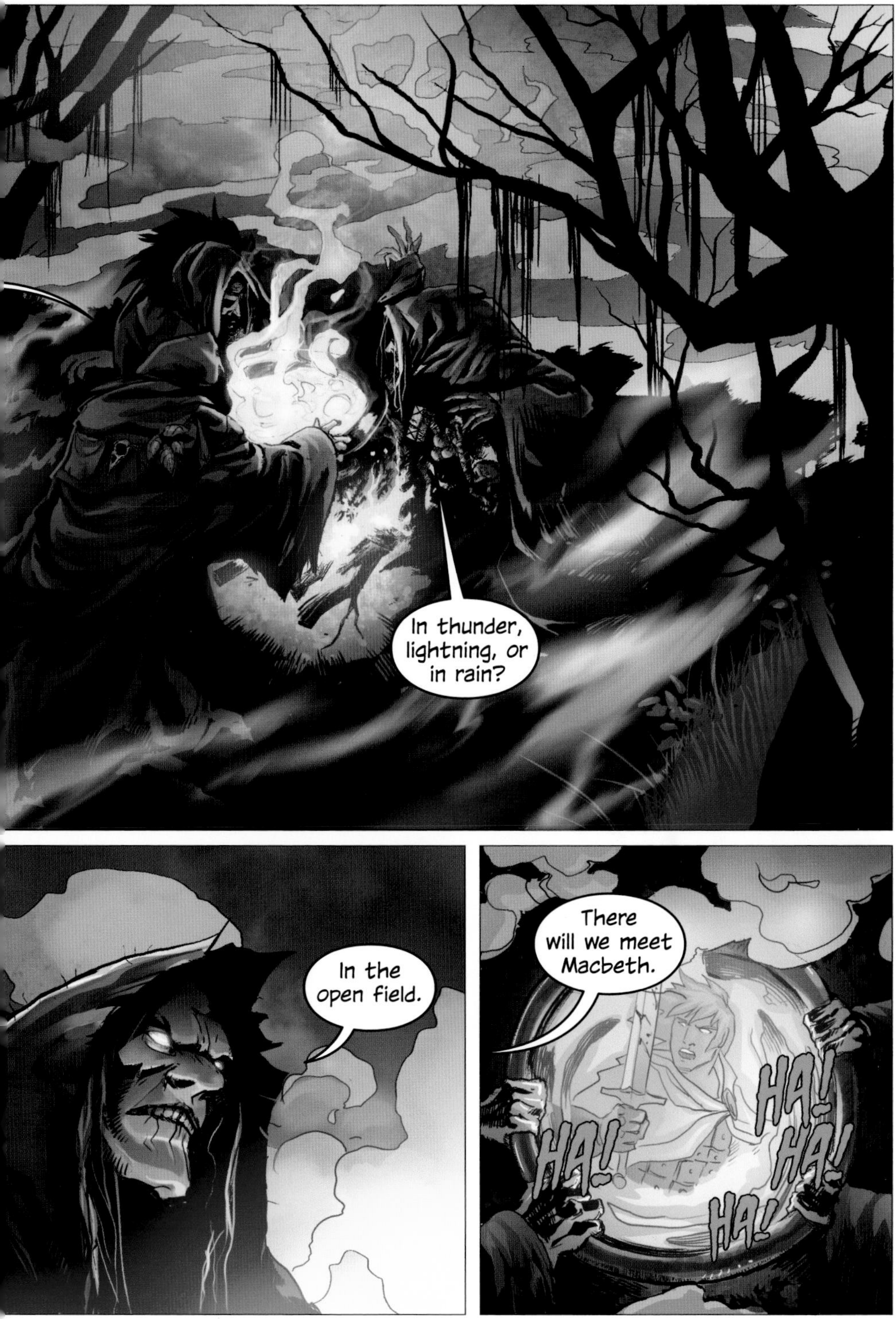

In thunder, lightning, or in rain?
In the open field.
There will we meet Macbeth.
HA! HA! HA! HA!

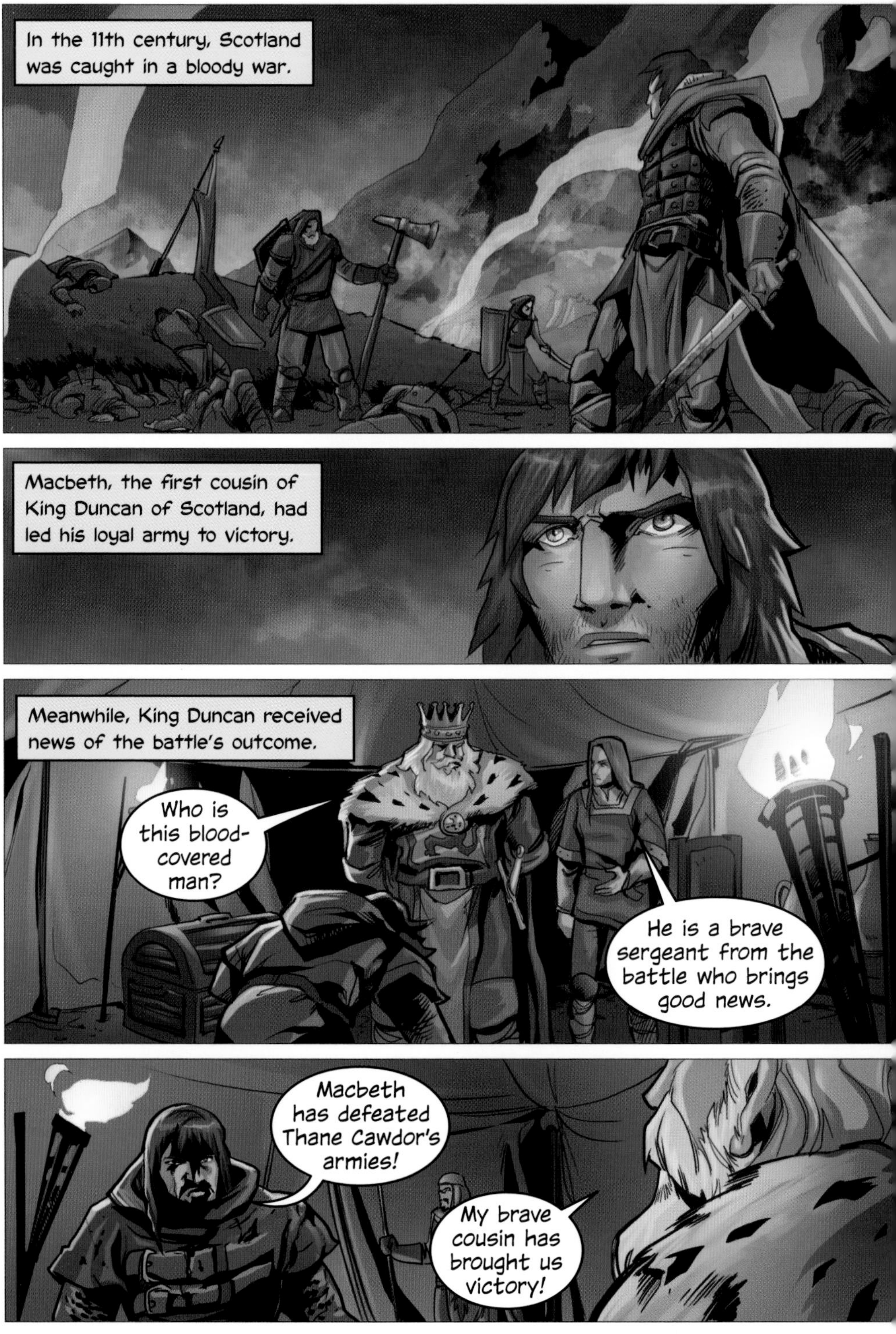
In the 11th century, Scotland was caught in a bloody war.
Macbeth, the first cousin of King Duncan of Scotland, had led his loyal army to victory.
Meanwhile, King Duncan received news of the battle's outcome.
Who is this blood-covered man?
He is a brave sergeant from the battle who brings good news.
Macbeth has defeated Thane Cawdor's armies!
My brave cousin has brought us victory!

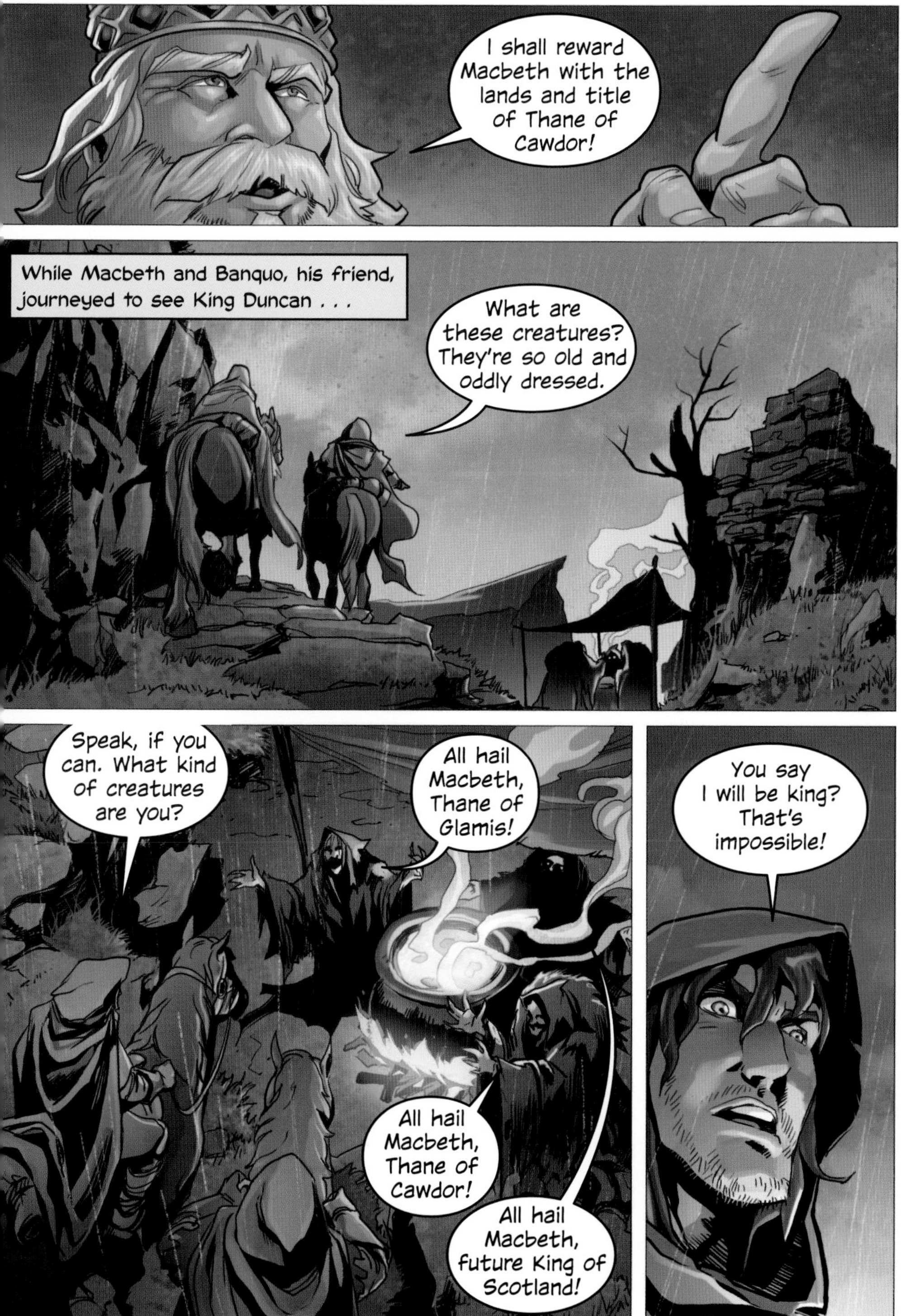
I shall reward Macbeth with the lands and title of Thane of Cawdor!
While Macbeth and Banquo, his friend, journeyed to see King Duncan . . .
What are these creatures? They're so old and oddly dressed.
Speak, if you can. What kind of creatures are you?
All hail Macbeth, Thane of Glamis!
All hail Macbeth, Thane of Cawdor!
All hail Macbeth, future King of Scotland!
You say I will be king? That's impossible!

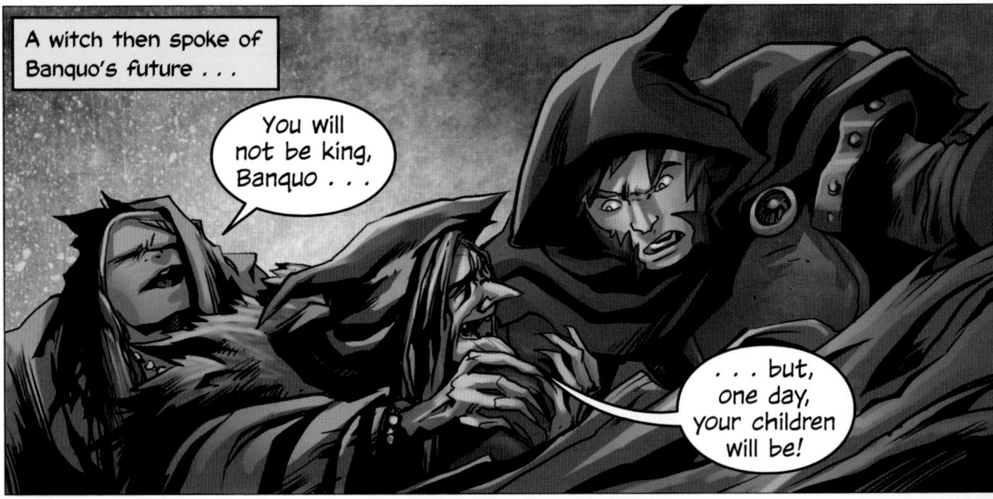
A witch then spoke of Banquo's future . . .
You will not be king, Banquo . . .
. . . but, one day, your children will be!

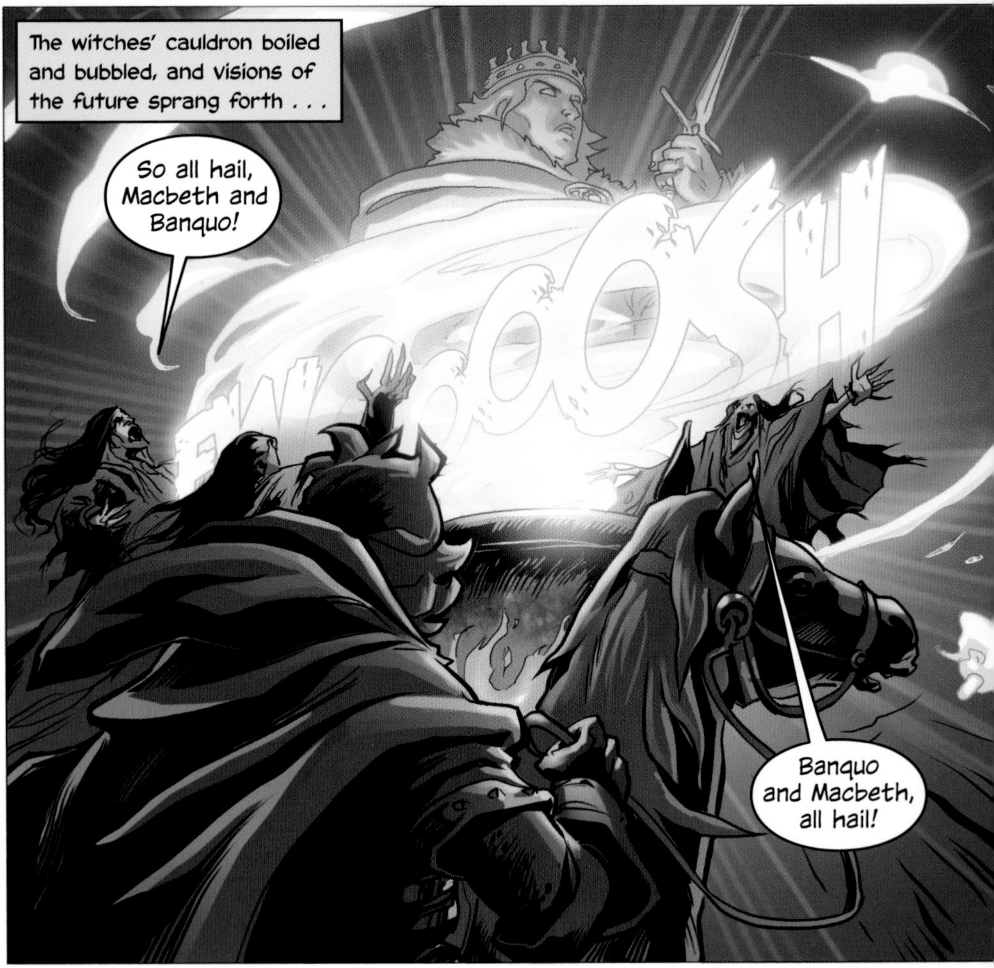
The witches' cauldron boiled and bubbled, and visions of the future sprang forth . . .
So all hail, Macbeth and Banquo!
FWOOOOSH
Banquo and Macbeth, all hail!

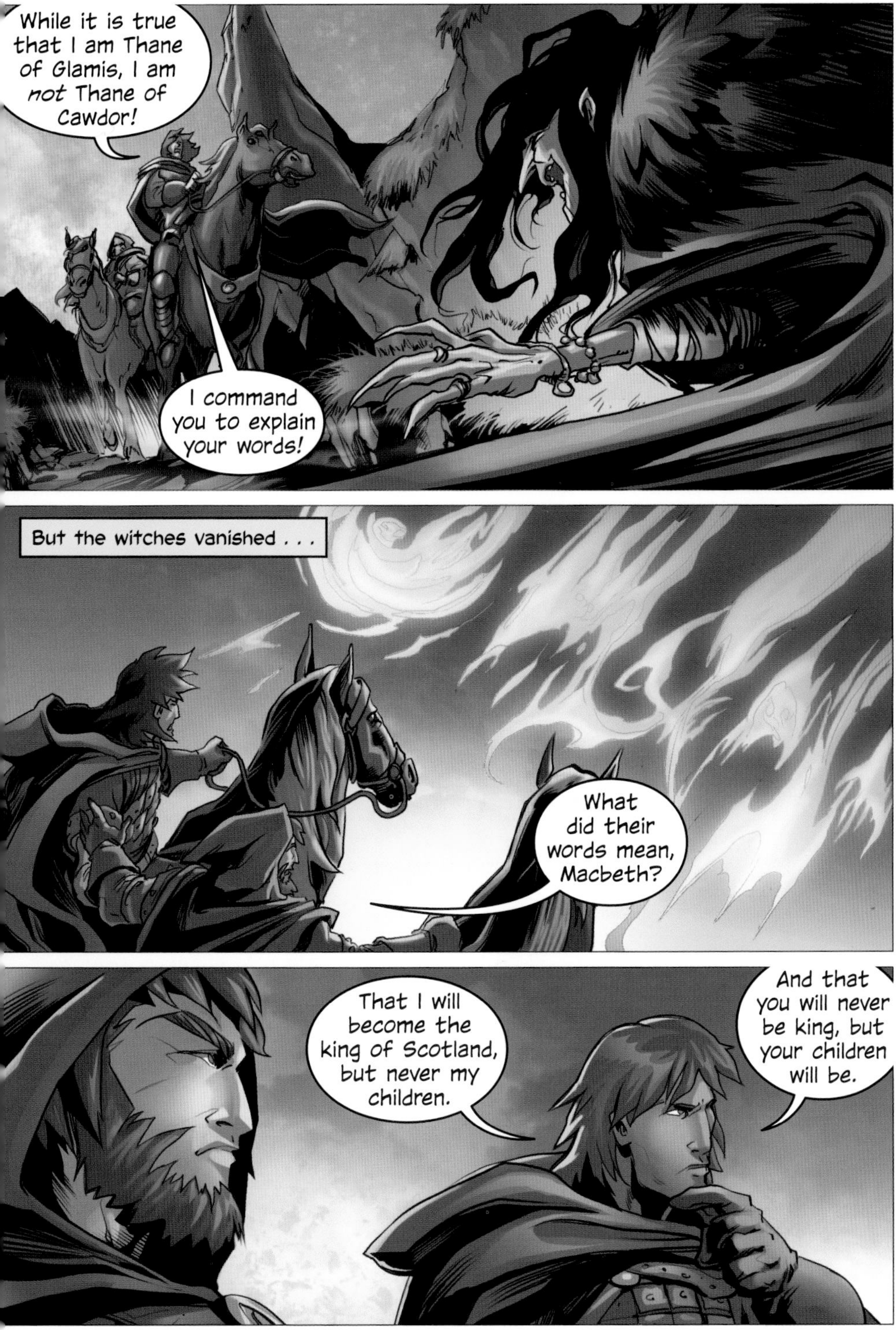
While it is true that I am Thane of Glamis, I am *not* Thane of Cawdor!
I command you to explain your words!
But the witches vanished . . .
What did their words mean, Macbeth?
That I will become the king of Scotland, but never my children.
And that you will never be king, but your children will be.

Later, in King Duncan's camp, Macbeth was greeted with joy.

Welcome home, my worthy cousin!

You have done so much for me by winning this war. I owe you more than I can ever repay.

Serving you is its own reward, my King.

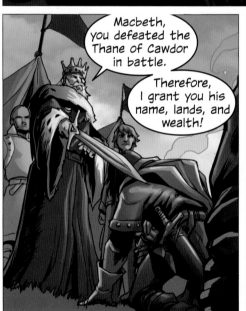

Macbeth, you defeated the Thane of Cawdor in battle.

Therefore, I grant you his name, lands, and wealth!

Arise, Macbeth, now Thane of Cawdor!

The three witches' words have already come true!

And they also said I will become king . . . !

And so, a dark desire began to stir within Macbeth.

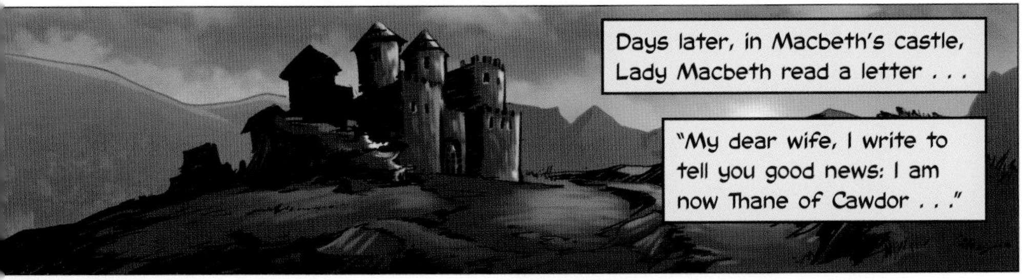
Days later, in Macbeth's castle, Lady Macbeth read a letter . . .
"My dear wife, I write to tell you good news: I am now Thane of Cawdor . . ."

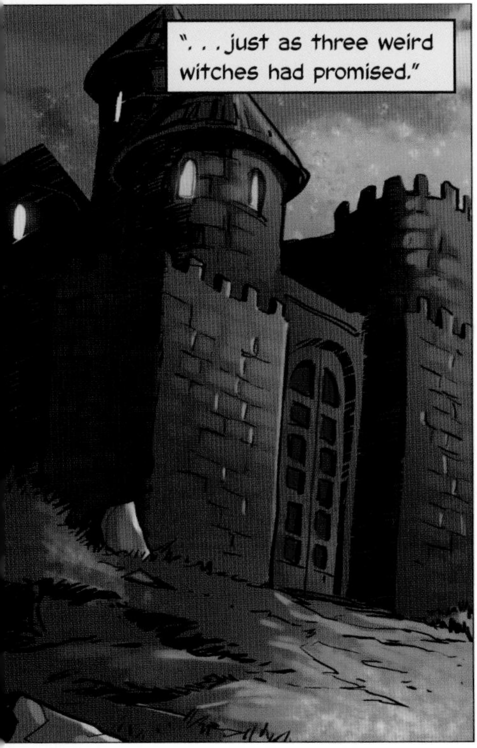
". . . just as three weird witches had promised."

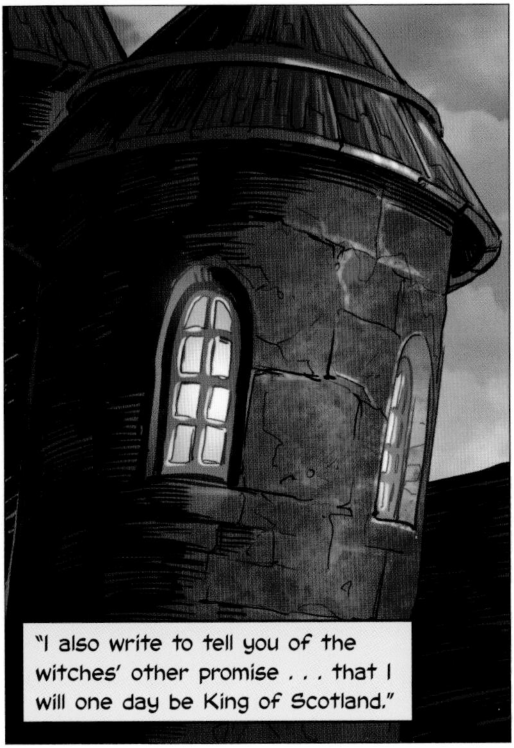
"I also write to tell you of the witches' other promise . . . that I will one day be King of Scotland."

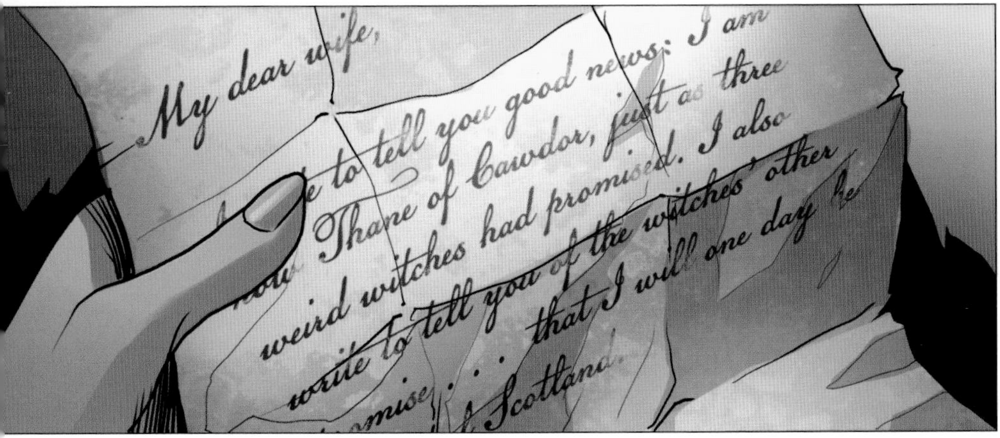
My dear wife,
to tell you good news: I am
Thane of Cawdor, just as three
weird witches had promised. I also
write to tell you of the witches' other
. . . that I will one day be
Scotland.

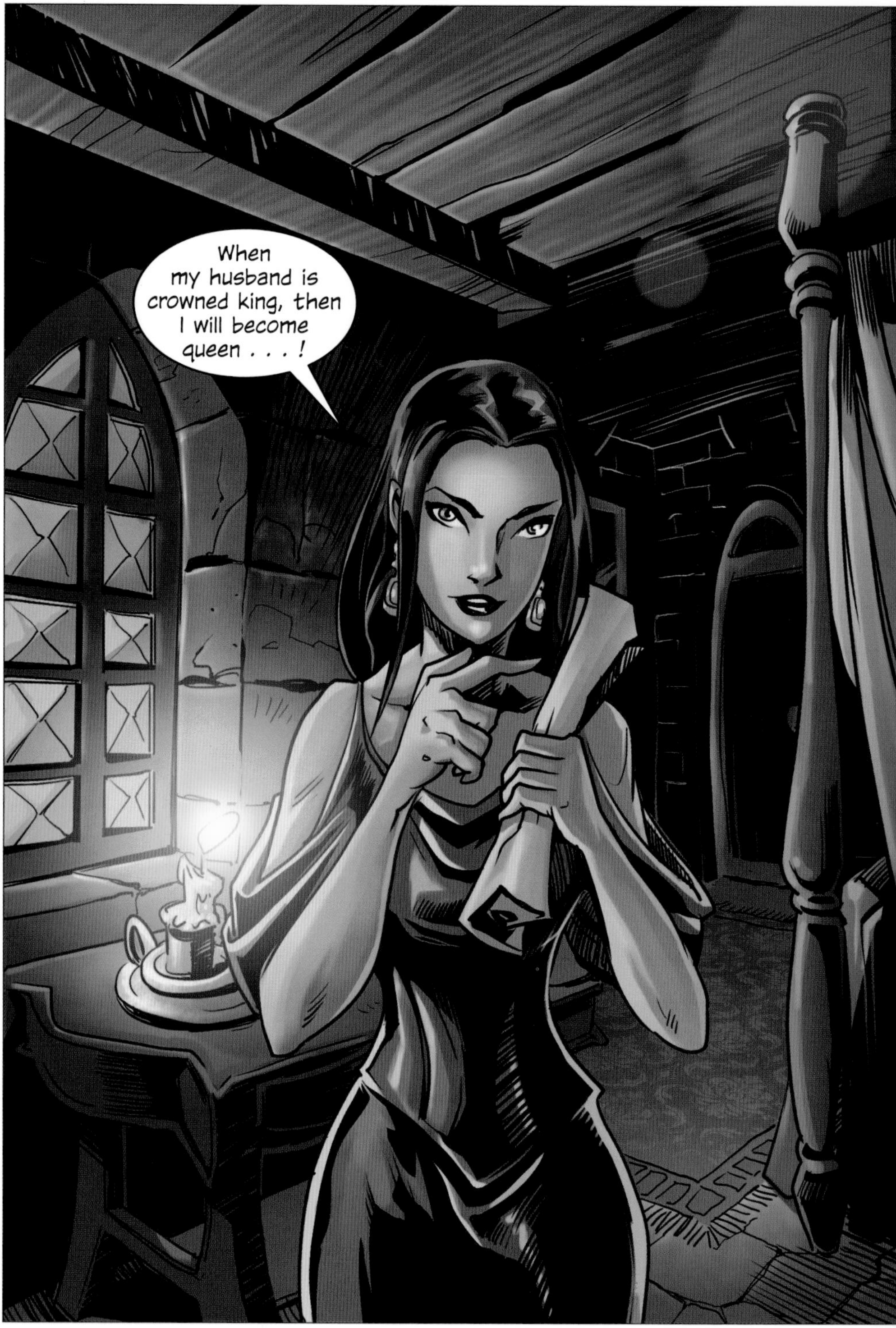
When my husband is crowned king, then I will become queen . . . !

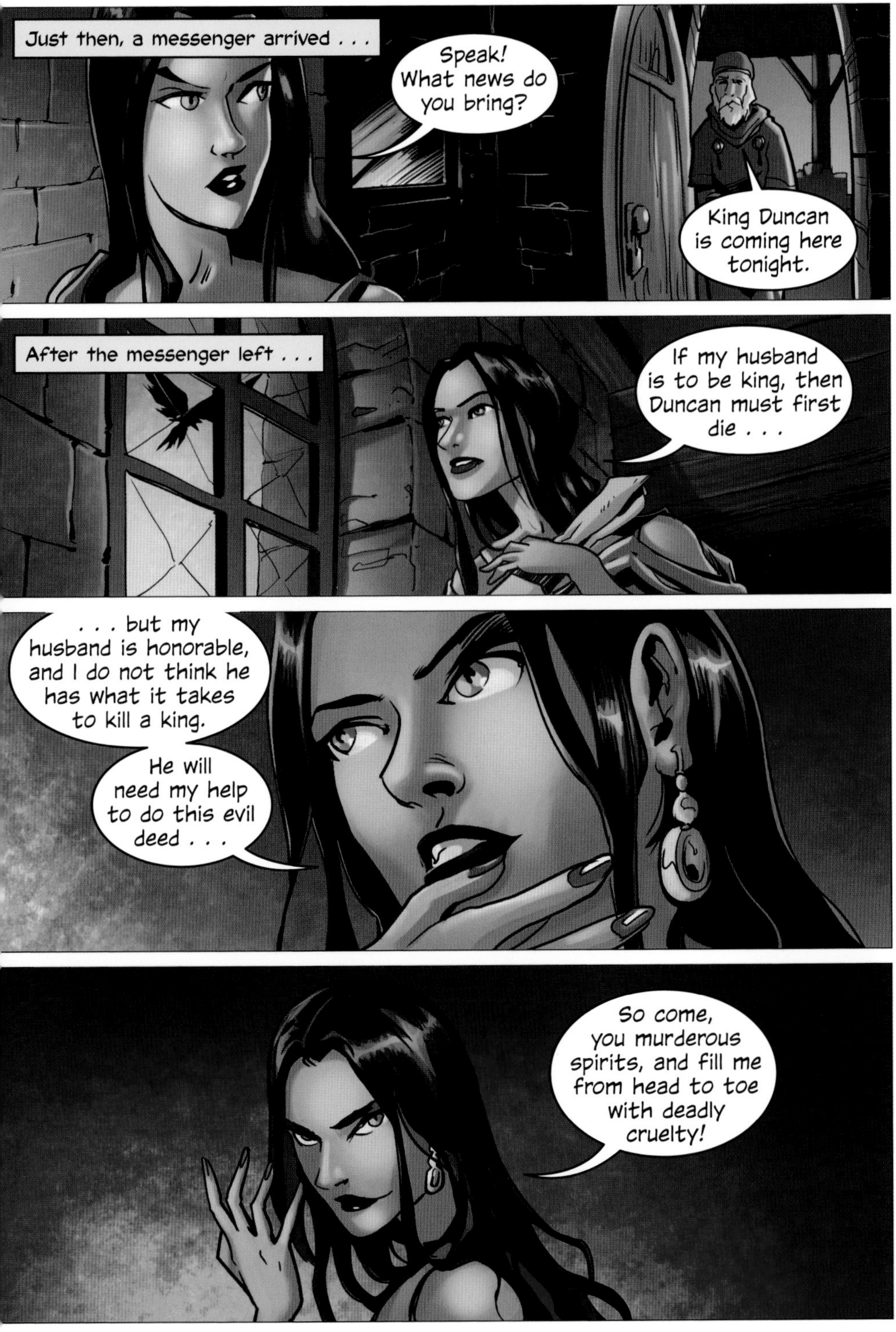
Just then, a messenger arrived . . .
Speak! What news do you bring?
King Duncan is coming here tonight.
After the messenger left . . .
If my husband is to be king, then Duncan must first die . . .
. . . but my husband is honorable, and I do not think he has what it takes to kill a king.
He will need my help to do this evil deed . . .
So come, you murderous spirits, and fill me from head to toe with deadly cruelty!

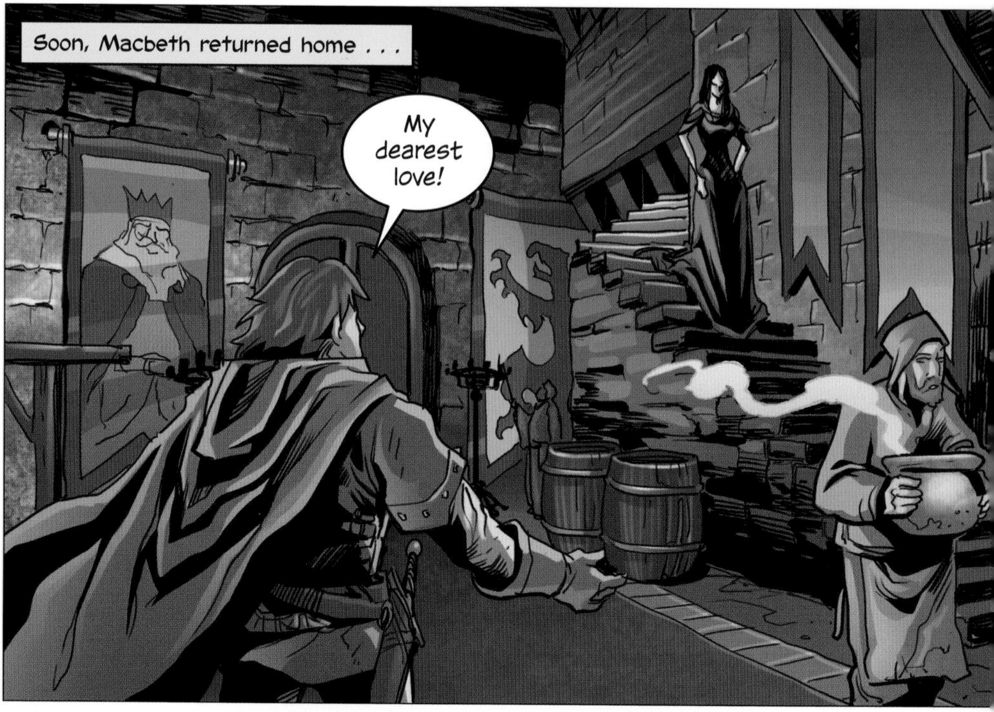
Soon, Macbeth returned home . . .
My dearest love!

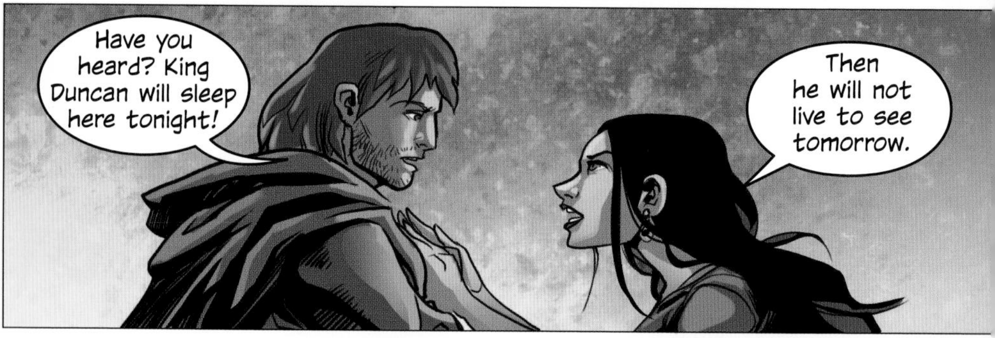
Have you heard? King Duncan will sleep here tonight!
Then he will not live to see tomorrow.

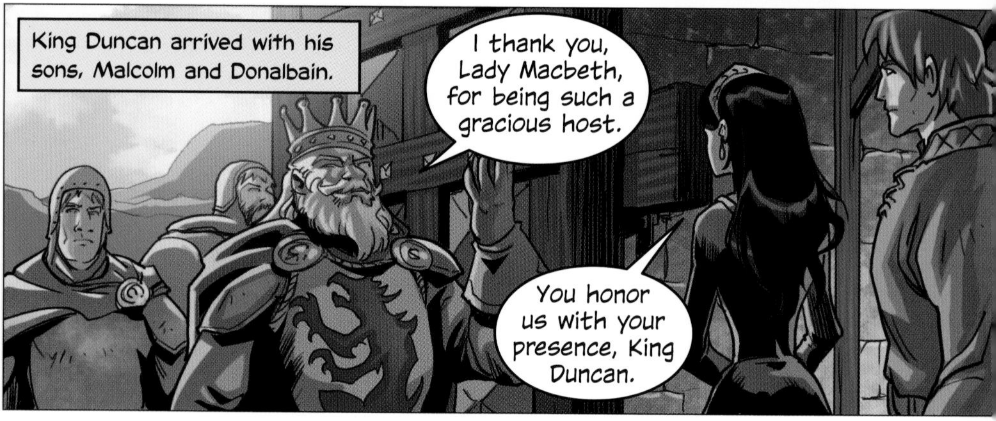
King Duncan arrived with his sons, Malcolm and Donalbain.
I thank you, Lady Macbeth, for being such a gracious host.
You honor us with your presence, King Duncan.

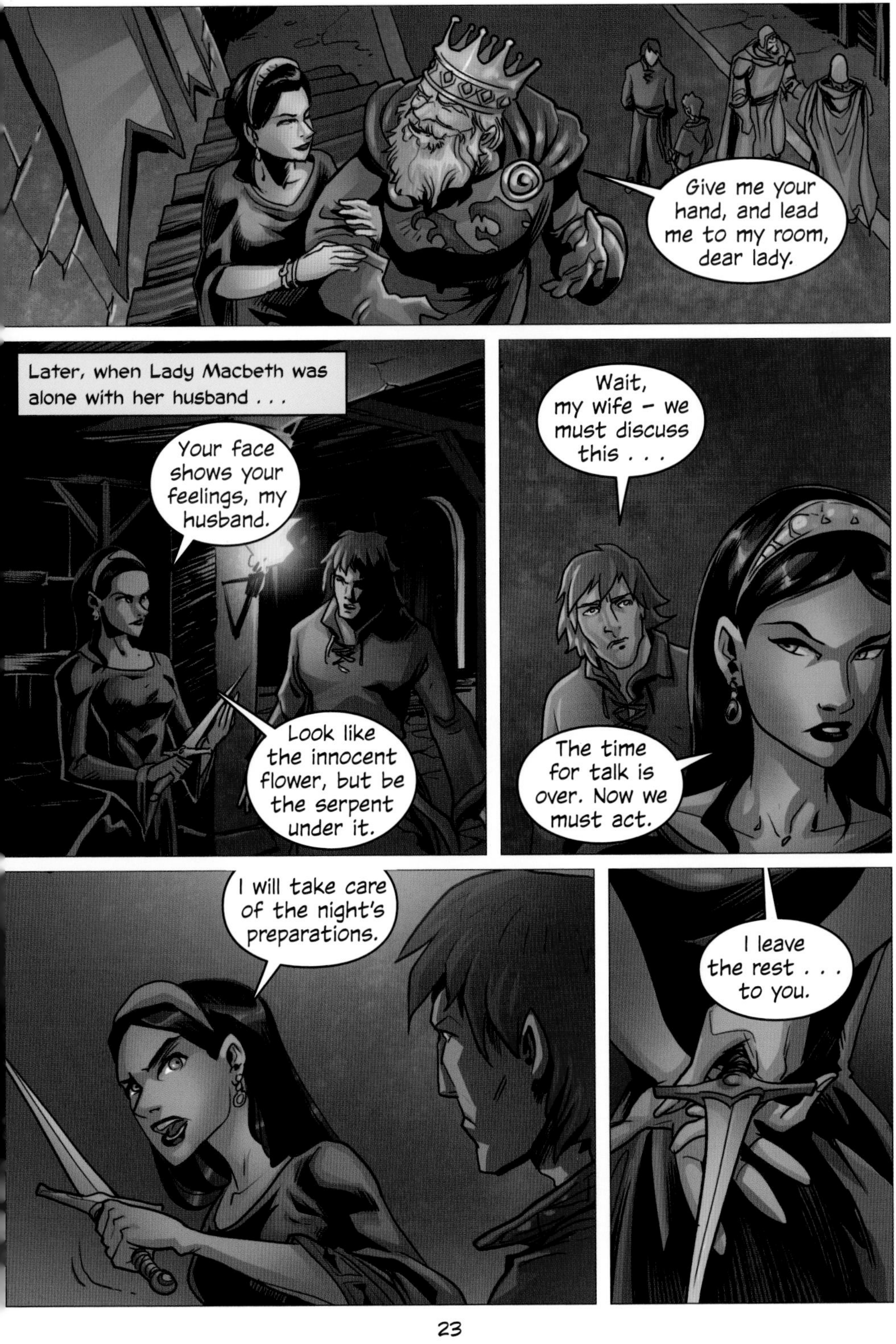

Give me your hand, and lead me to my room, dear lady.
Later, when Lady Macbeth was alone with her husband . . .
Your face shows your feelings, my husband.
Look like the innocent flower, but be the serpent under it.
Wait, my wife – we must discuss this . . .
The time for talk is over. Now we must act.
I will take care of the night's preparations.
I leave the rest . . . to you.

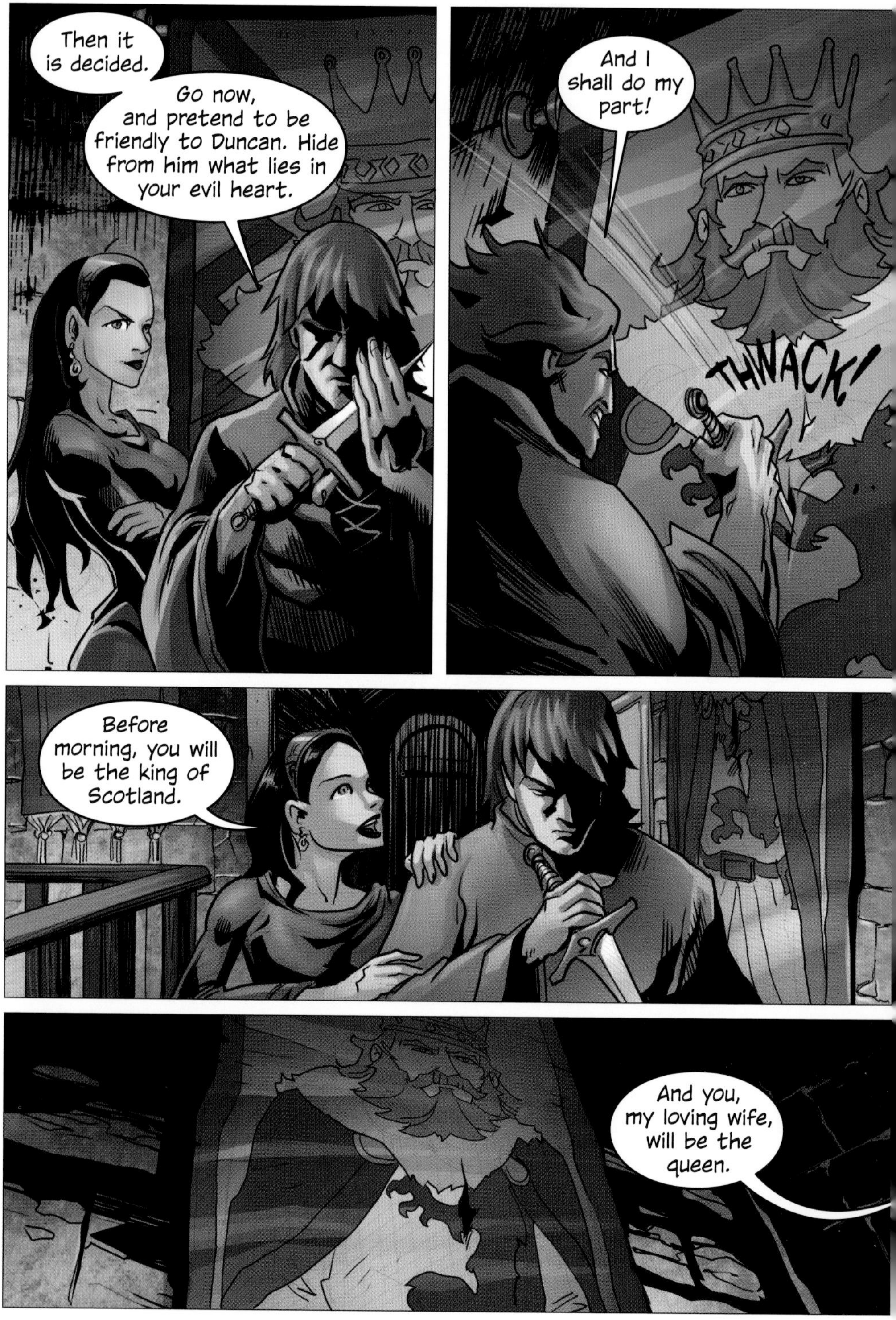
Then it is decided.
Go now, and pretend to be friendly to Duncan. Hide from him what lies in your evil heart.
And I shall do my part!
THWACK!
Before morning, you will be the king of Scotland.
And you, my loving wife, will be the queen.

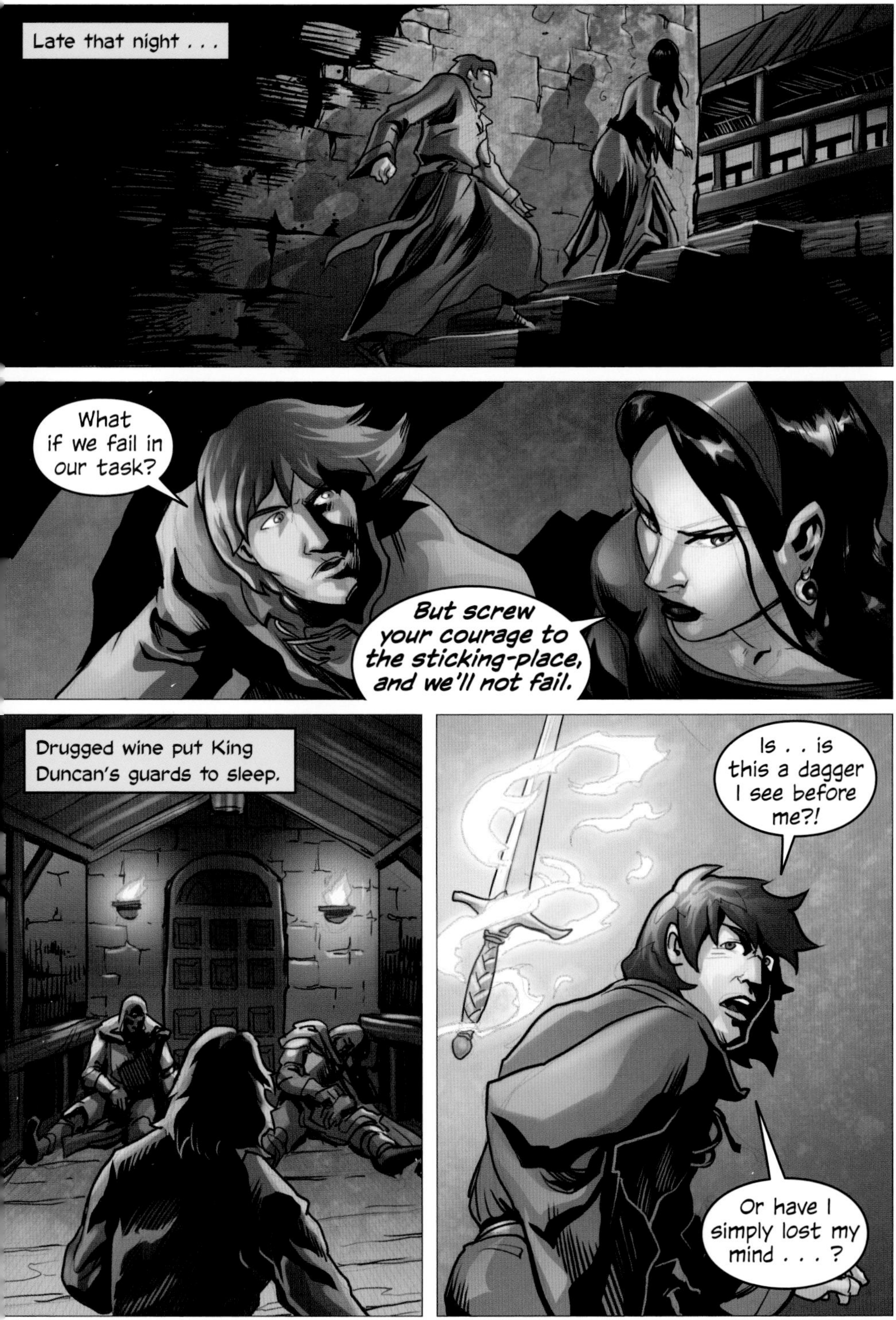
Late that night . . .
What if we fail in our task?
But screw your courage to the sticking-place, and we'll not fail.
Drugged wine put King Duncan's guards to sleep.
Is . . is this a dagger I see before me?!
Or have I simply lost my mind . . . ?

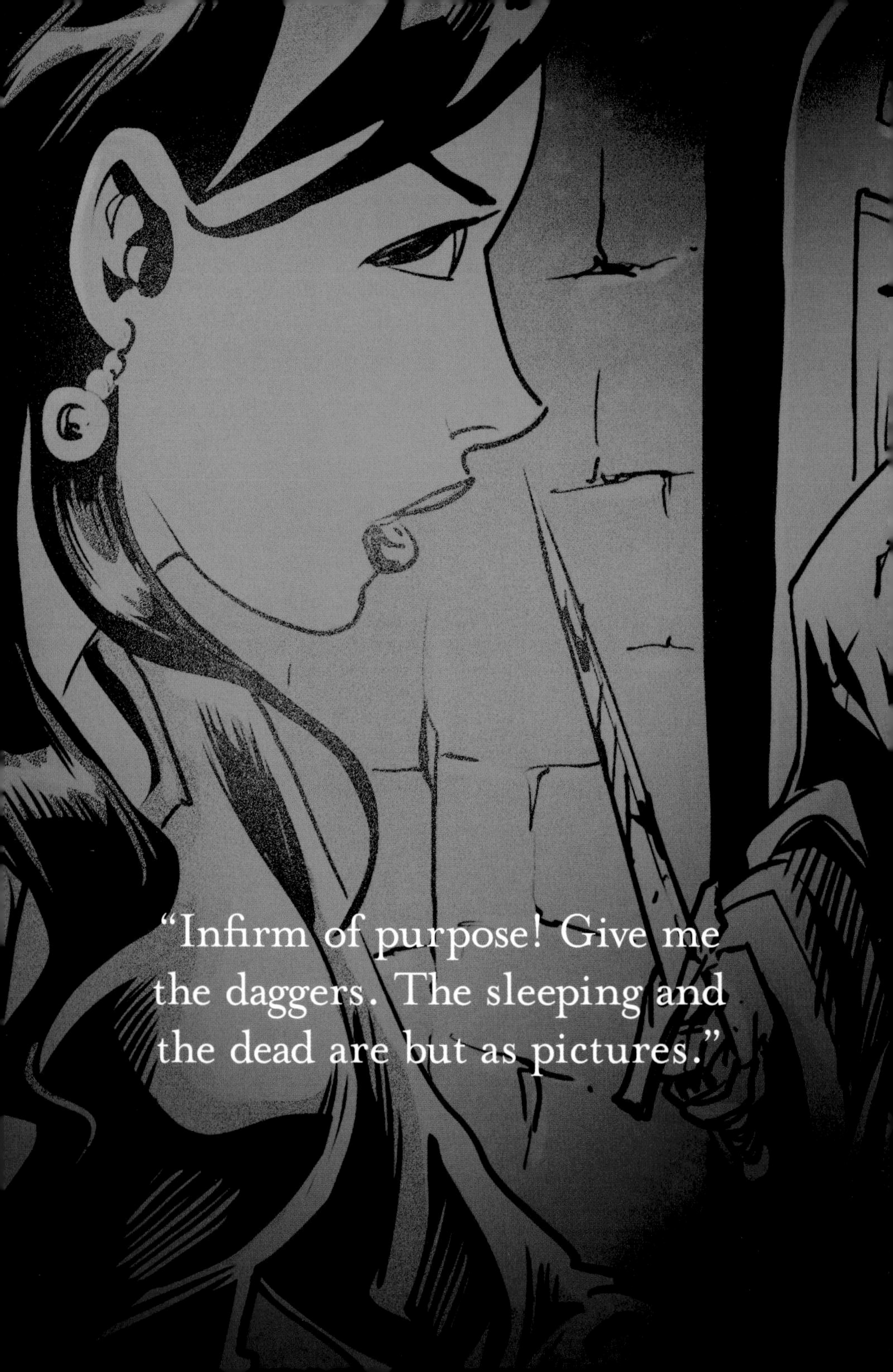
"Infirm of purpose! Give me the daggers. The sleeping and the dead are but as pictures."

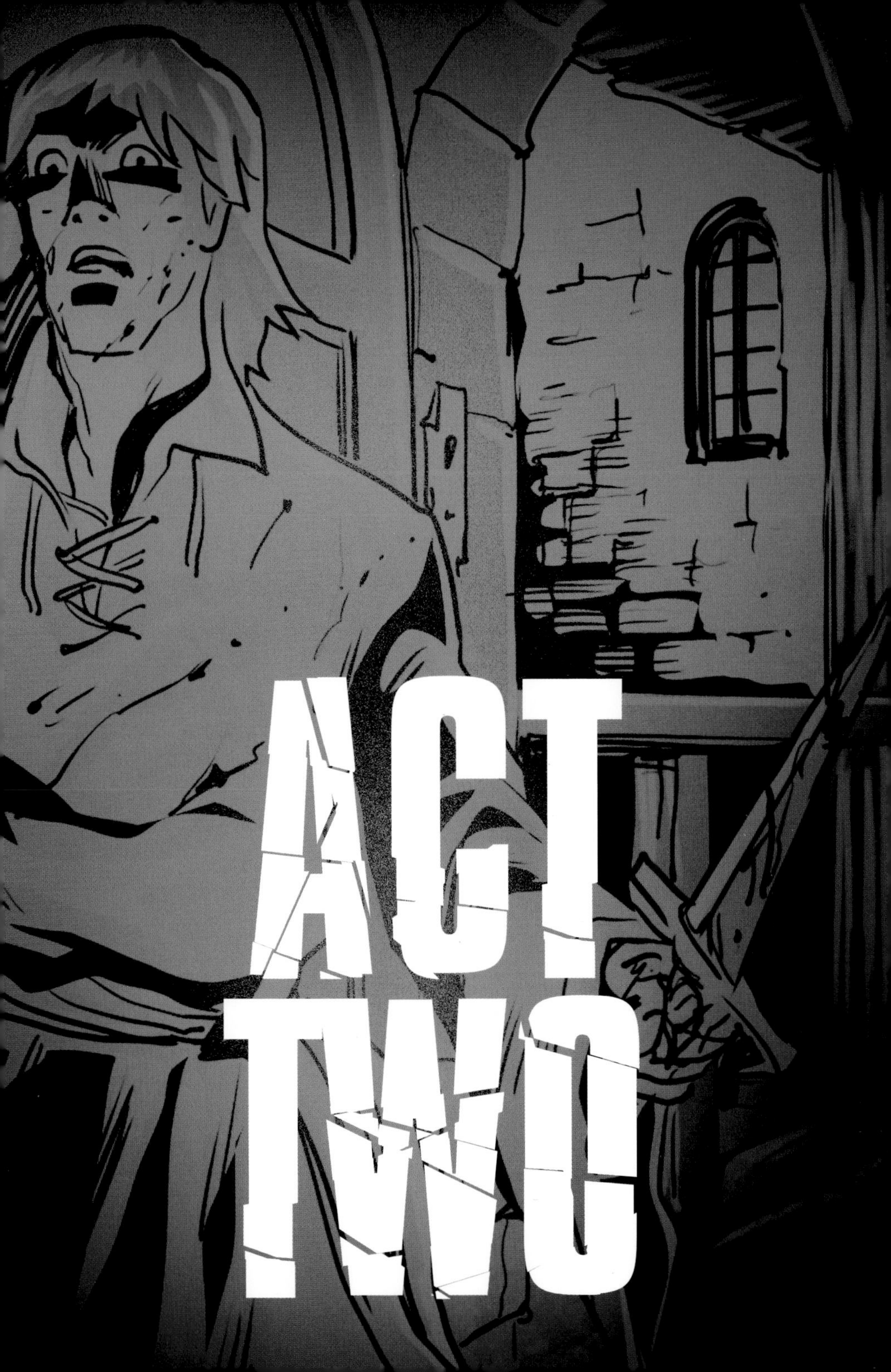
ACT
TWO

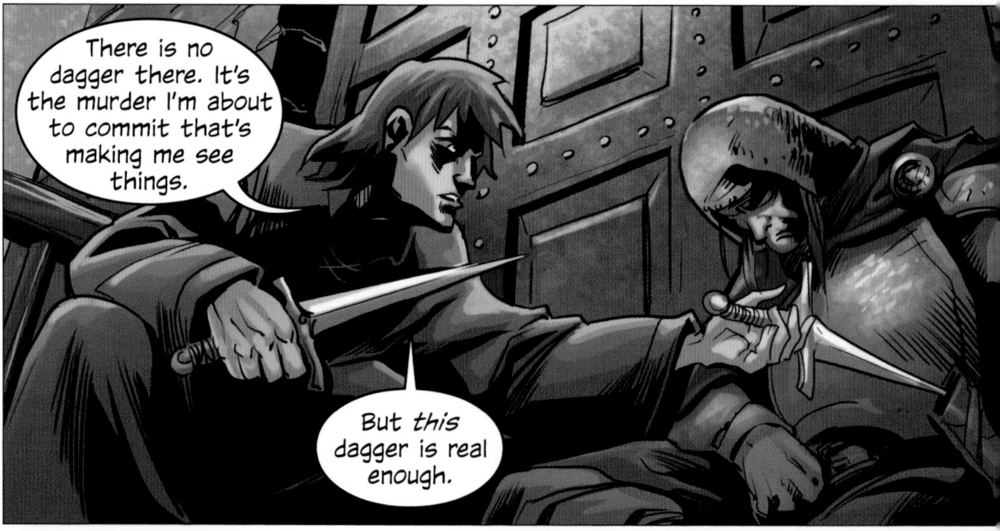
There is no dagger there. It's the murder I'm about to commit that's making me see things.
But *this* dagger is real enough.

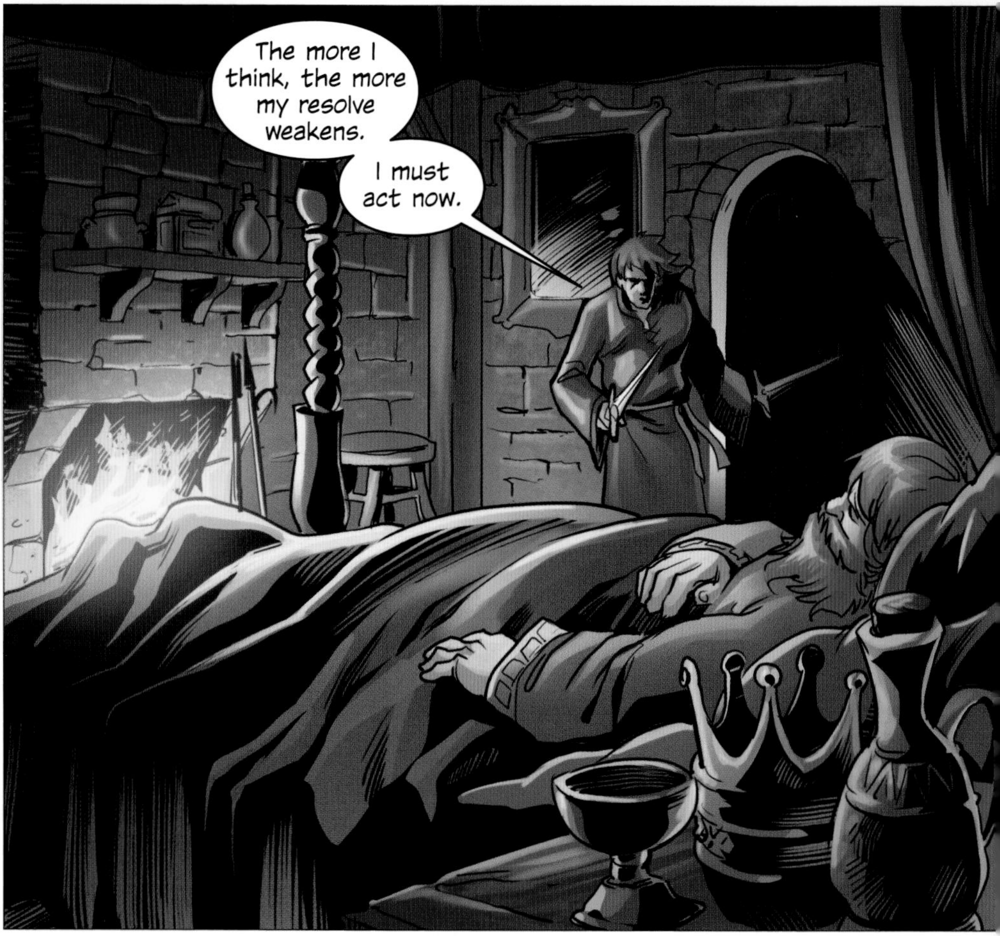
The more I think, the more my resolve weakens.
I must act now.

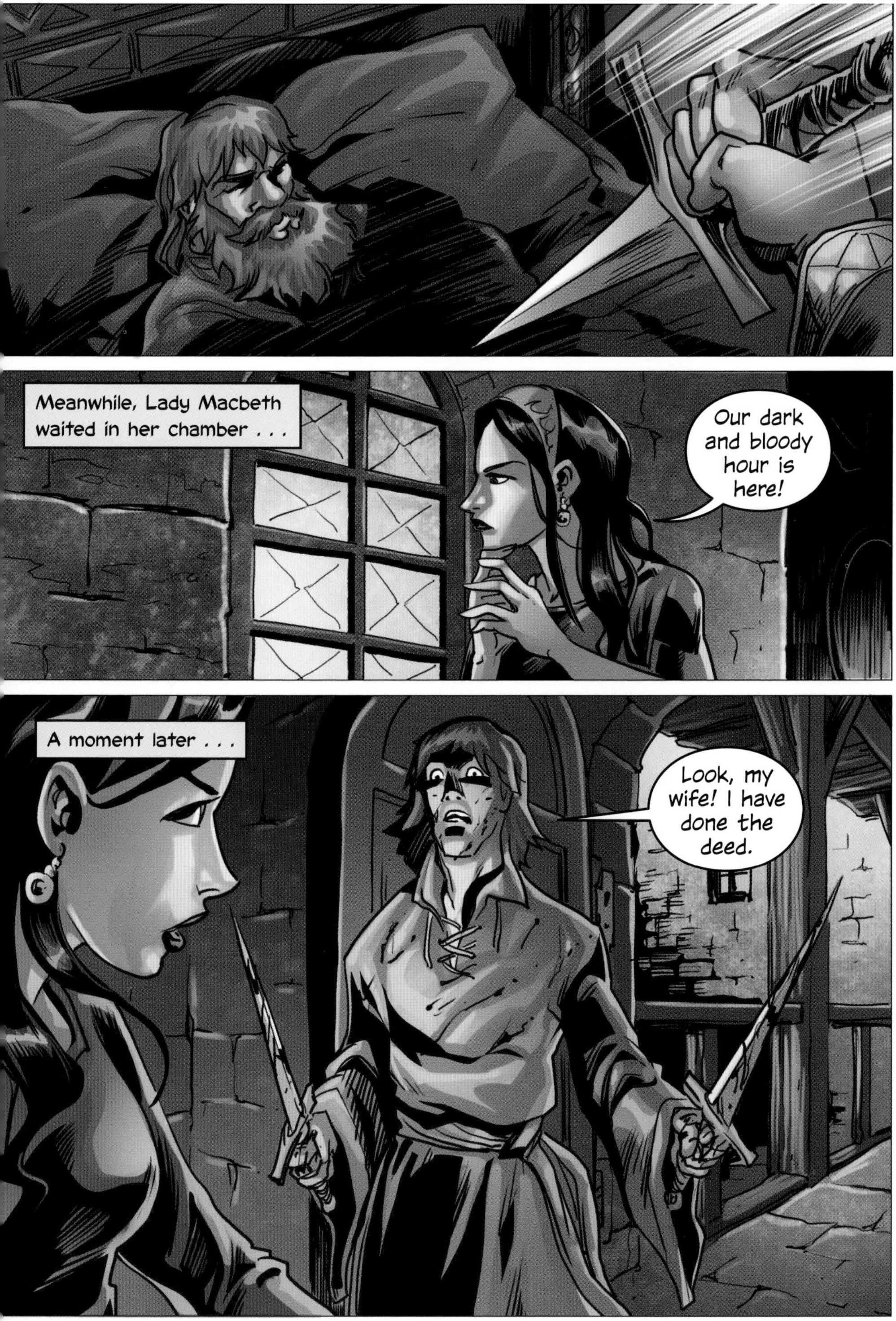
Meanwhile, Lady Macbeth waited in her chamber . . .
Our dark and bloody hour is here!
A moment later . . .
Look, my wife! I have done the deed.

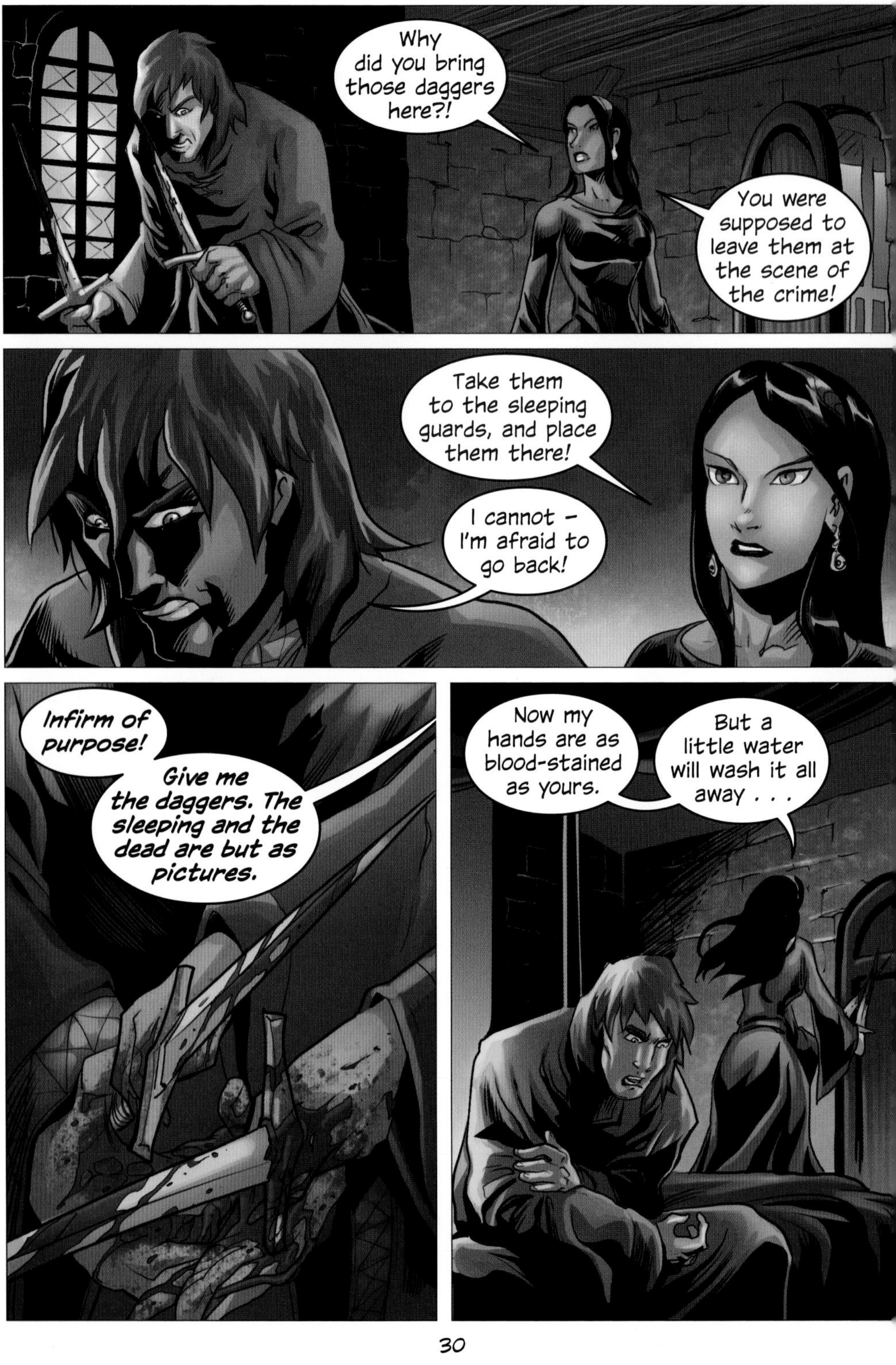
Why did you bring those daggers here?!
You were supposed to leave them at the scene of the crime!
Take them to the sleeping guards, and place them there!
I cannot - I'm afraid to go back!
Infirm of purpose!
Give me the daggers. The sleeping and the dead are but as pictures.
Now my hands are as blood-stained as yours.
But a little water will wash it all away . . .

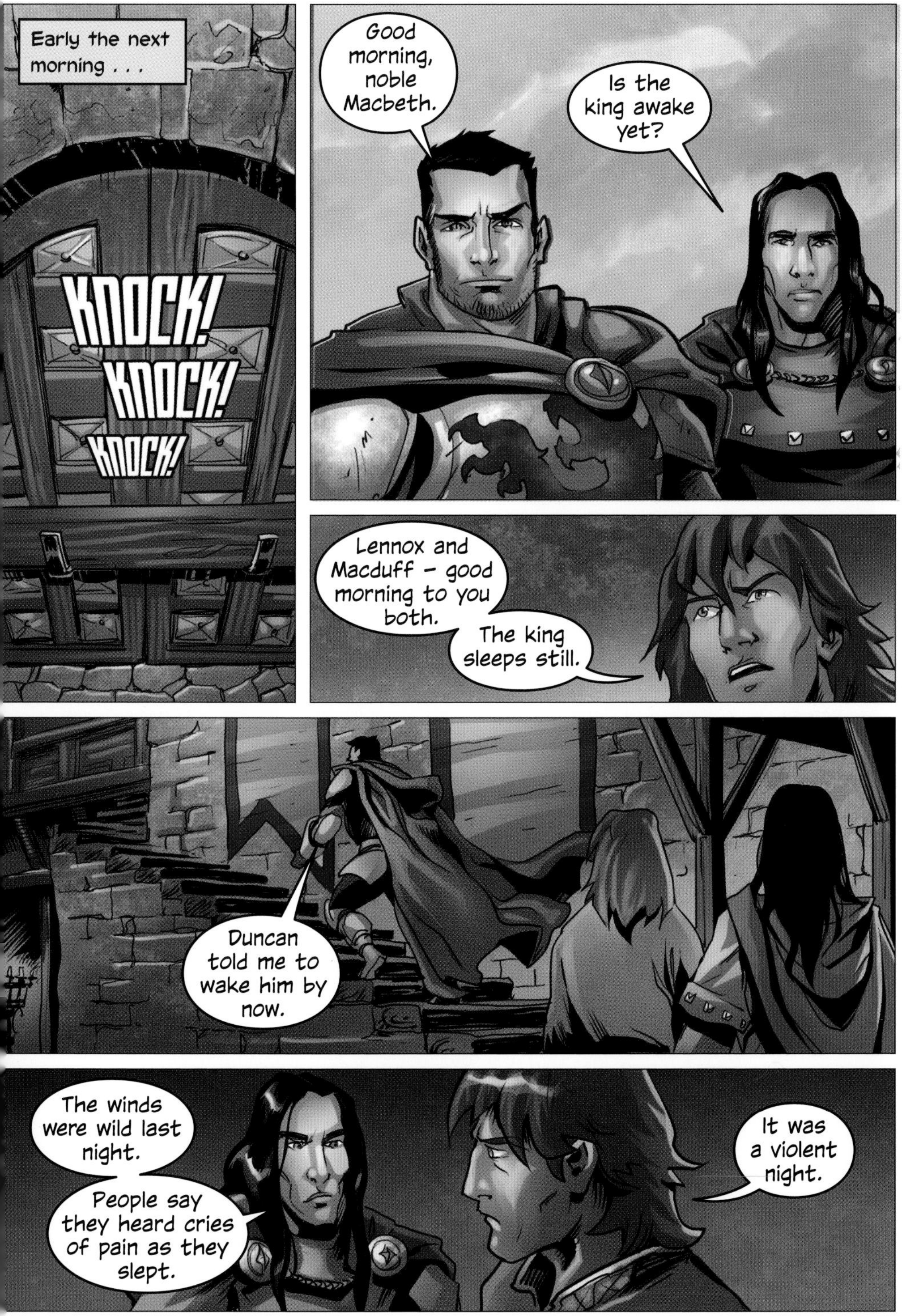
Early the next morning . . .
KNOCK! KNOCK! KNOCK!
Good morning, noble Macbeth.
Is the king awake yet?
Lennox and Macduff - good morning to you both.
The king sleeps still.
Duncan told me to wake him by now.
The winds were wild last night.
People say they heard cries of pain as they slept.
It was a violent night.

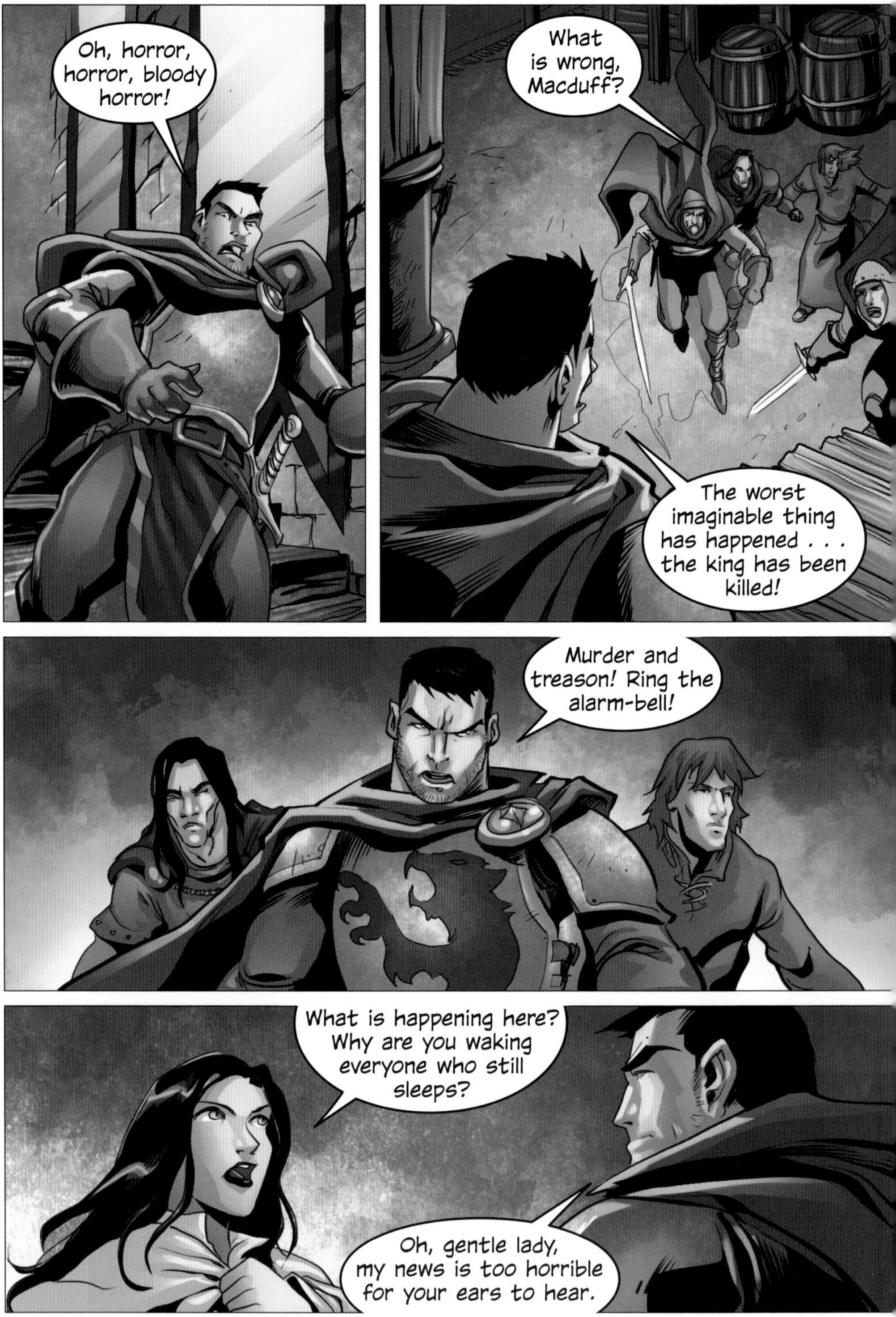
Oh, horror, horror, bloody horror!
What is wrong, Macduff?
The worst imaginable thing has happened . . . the king has been killed!
Murder and treason! Ring the alarm-bell!
What is happening here? Why are you waking everyone who still sleeps?
Oh, gentle lady, my news is too horrible for your ears to hear.

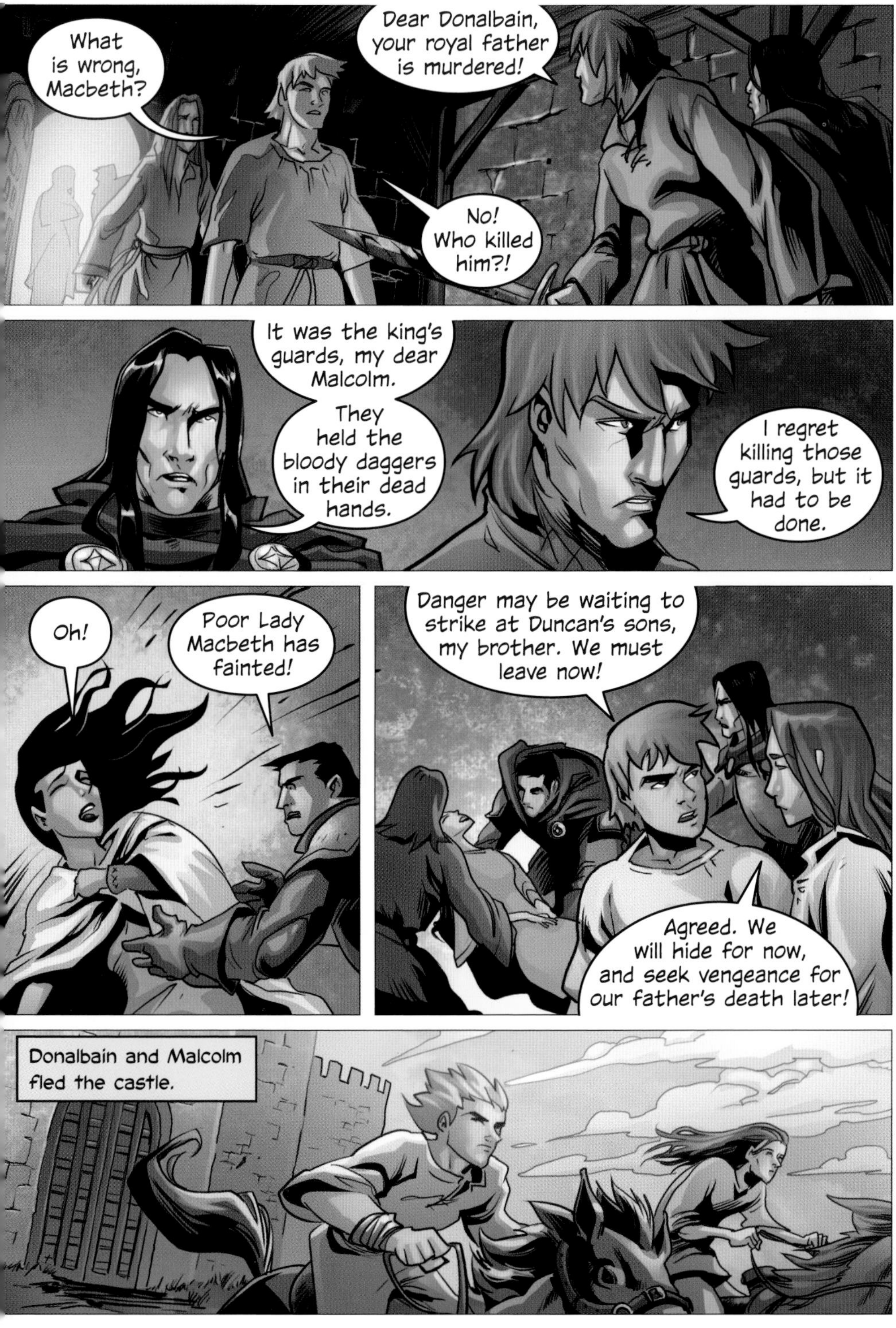
What is wrong, Macbeth?
Dear Donalbain, your royal father is murdered!
No! Who killed him?!
It was the king's guards, my dear Malcolm.
They held the bloody daggers in their dead hands.
I regret killing those guards, but it had to be done.
Oh!
Poor Lady Macbeth has fainted!
Danger may be waiting to strike at Duncan's sons, my brother. We must leave now!
Agreed. We will hide for now, and seek vengeance for our father's death later!
Donalbain and Malcolm fled the castle.

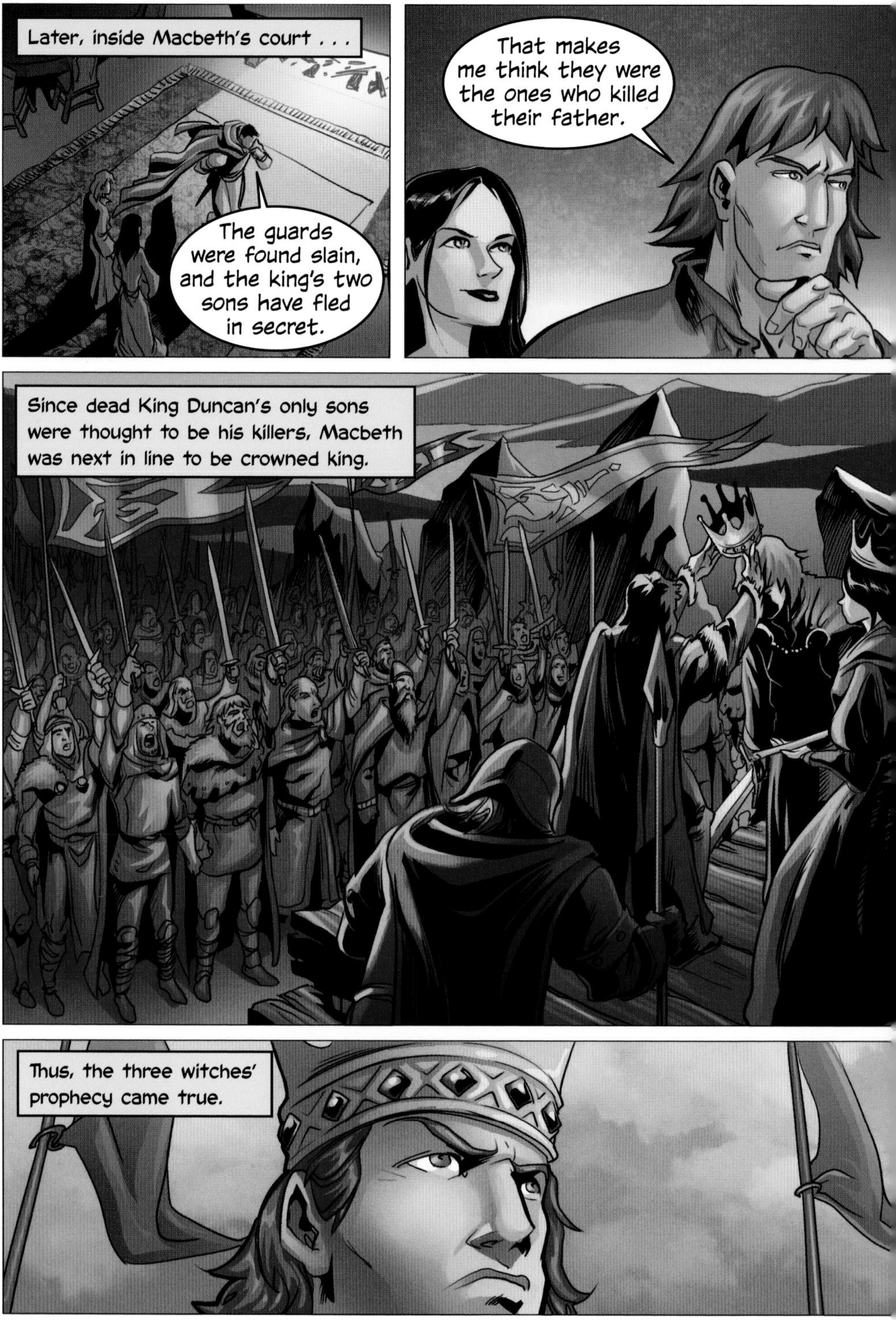
Later, inside Macbeth's court . . .
The guards were found slain, and the king's two sons have fled in secret.
That makes me think they were the ones who killed their father.
Since dead King Duncan's only sons were thought to be his killers, Macbeth was next in line to be crowned king.
Thus, the three witches' prophecy came true.

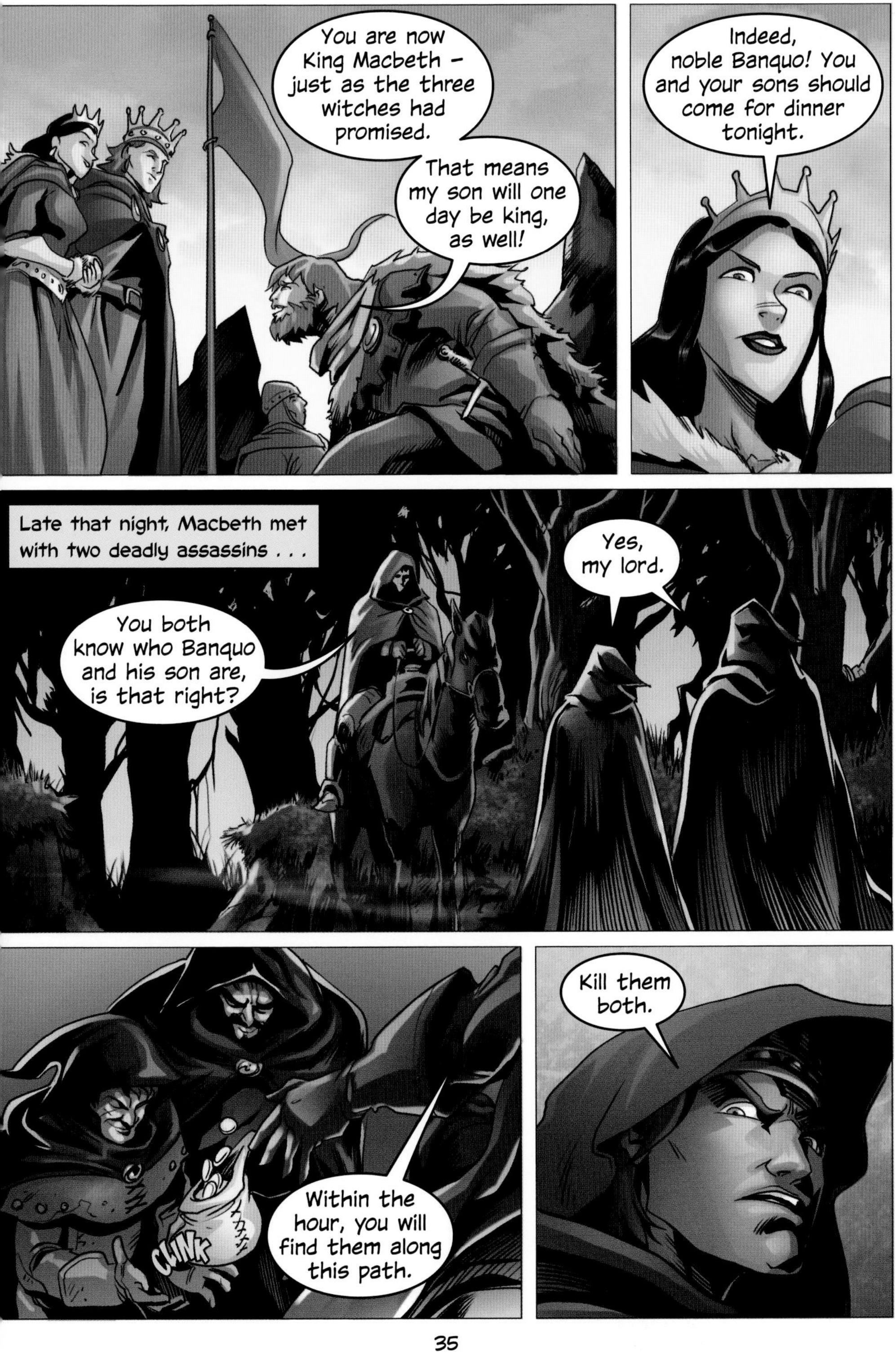
You are now King Macbeth – just as the three witches had promised.
That means my son will one day be king, as well!
Indeed, noble Banquo! You and your sons should come for dinner tonight.
Late that night, Macbeth met with two deadly assassins . . .
You both know who Banquo and his son are, is that right?
Yes, my lord.
Within the hour, you will find them along this path.
CLINK
Kill them both.

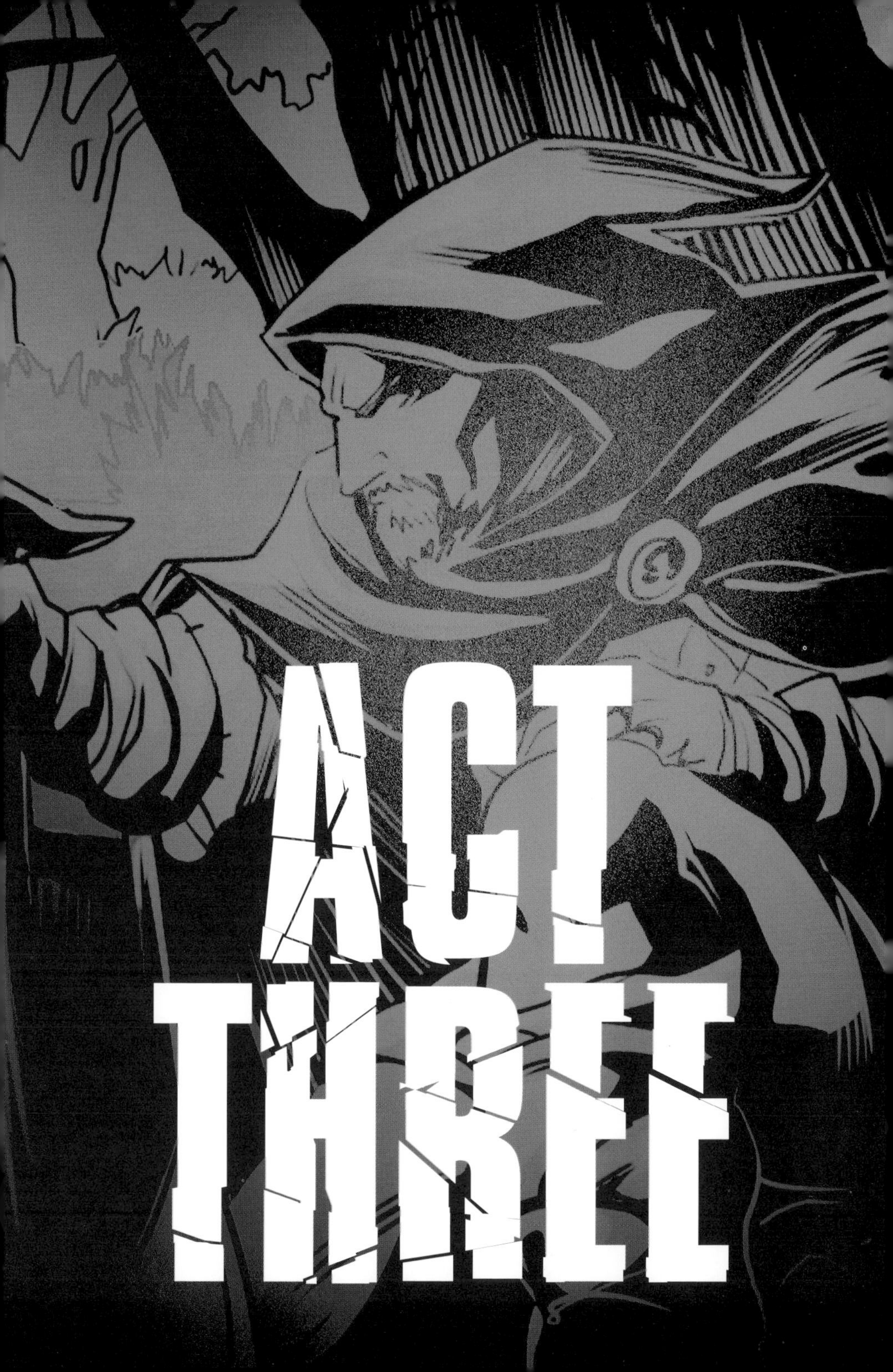
ACT
THREE

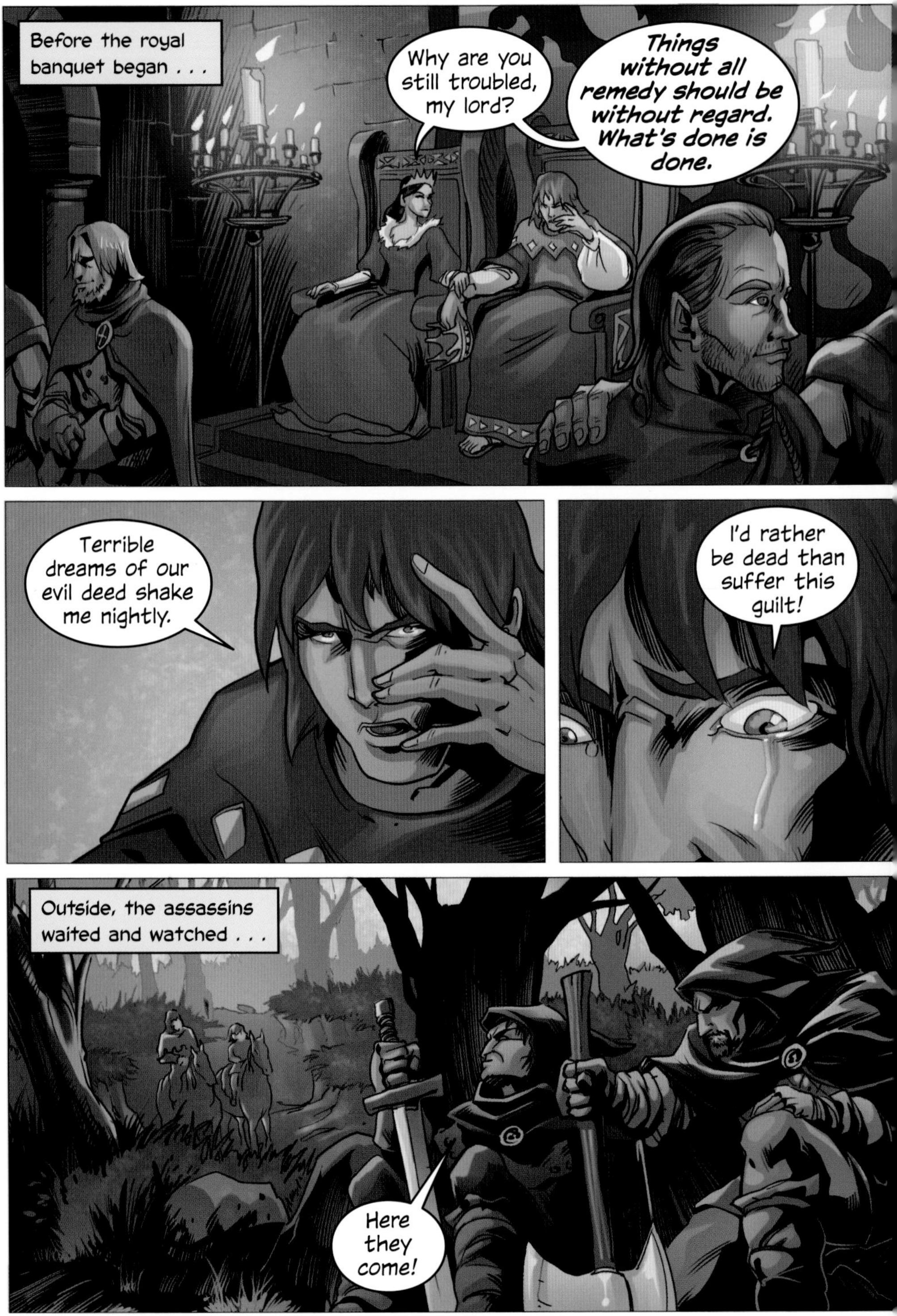
Before the royal banquet began . . .
Why are you still troubled, my lord?
Things without all remedy should be without regard. What's done is done.
Terrible dreams of our evil deed shake me nightly.
I'd rather be dead than suffer this guilt!
Outside, the assassins waited and watched . . .
Here they come!

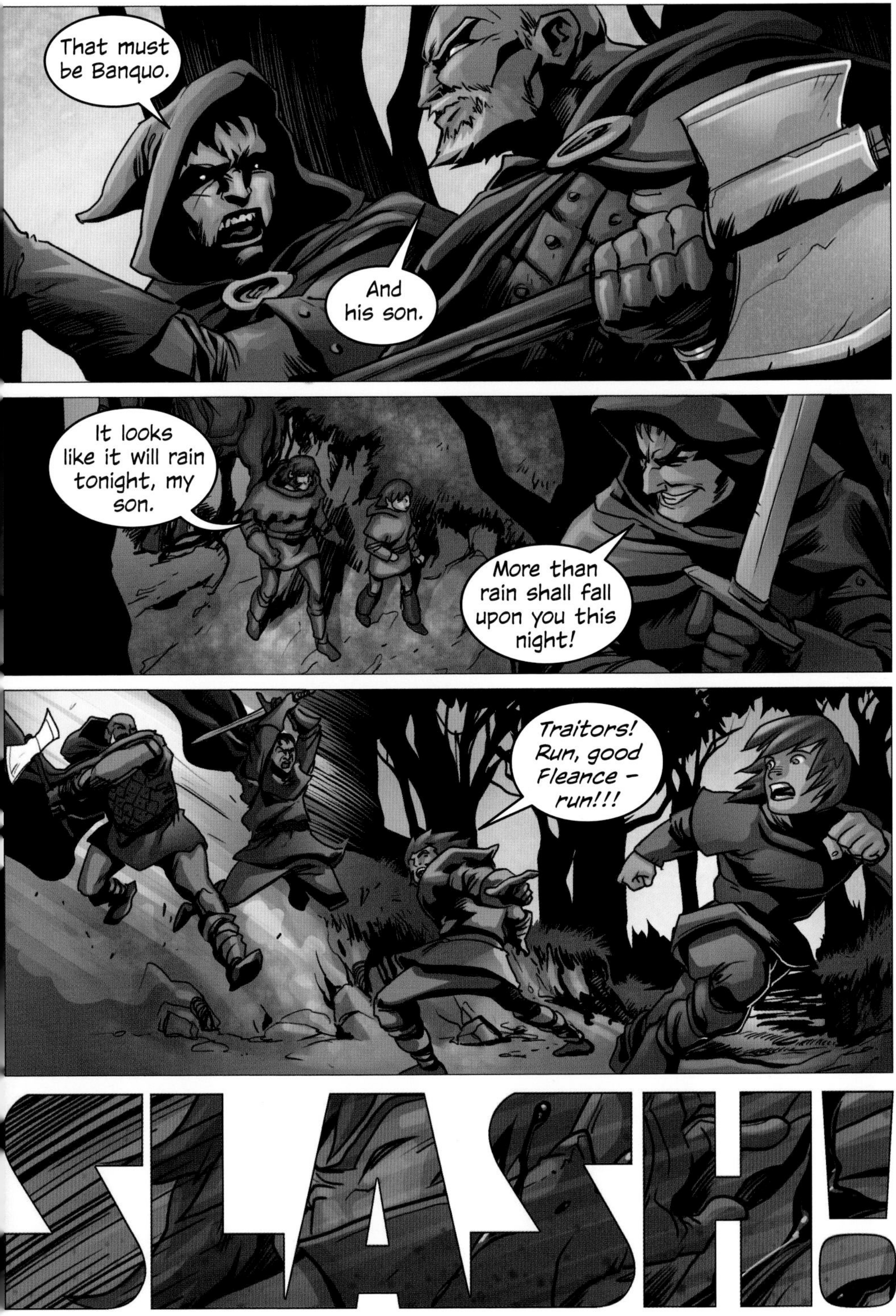
That must be Banquo.
And his son.
It looks like it will rain tonight, my son.
More than rain shall fall upon you this night!
Traitors! Run, good Fleance - run!!!
SLASH!

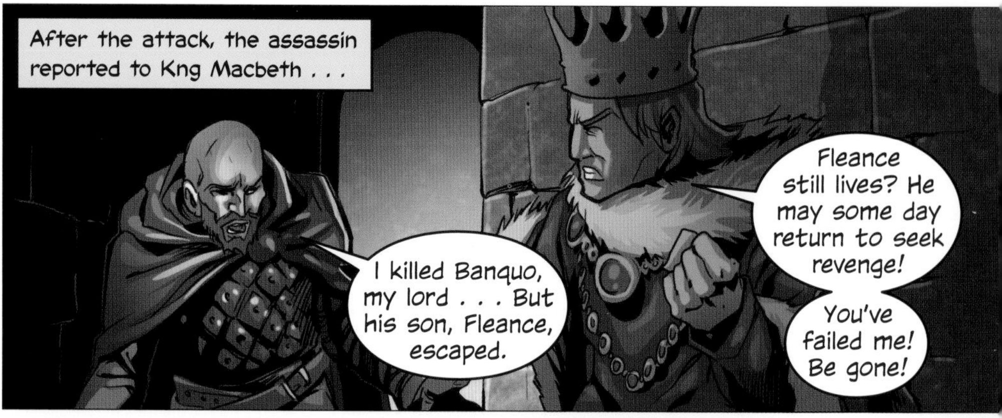
After the attack, the assassin reported to Kng Macbeth . . .
I killed Banquo, my lord . . . But his son, Fleance, escaped.
Fleance still lives? He may some day return to seek revenge!
You've failed me! Be gone!

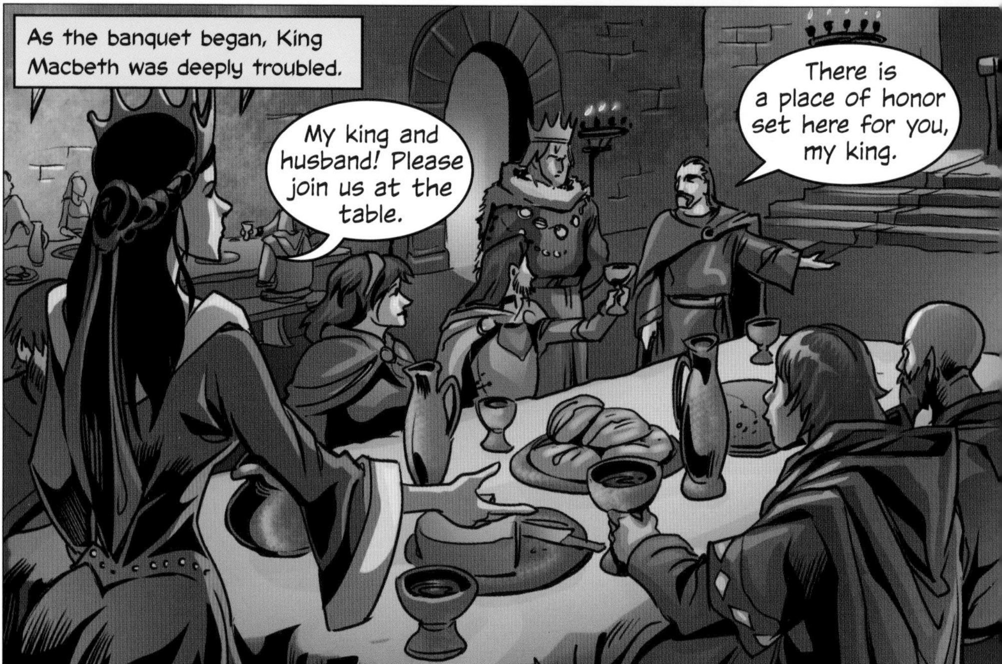
As the banquet began, King Macbeth was deeply troubled.
My king and husband! Please join us at the table.
There is a place of honor set here for you, my king.

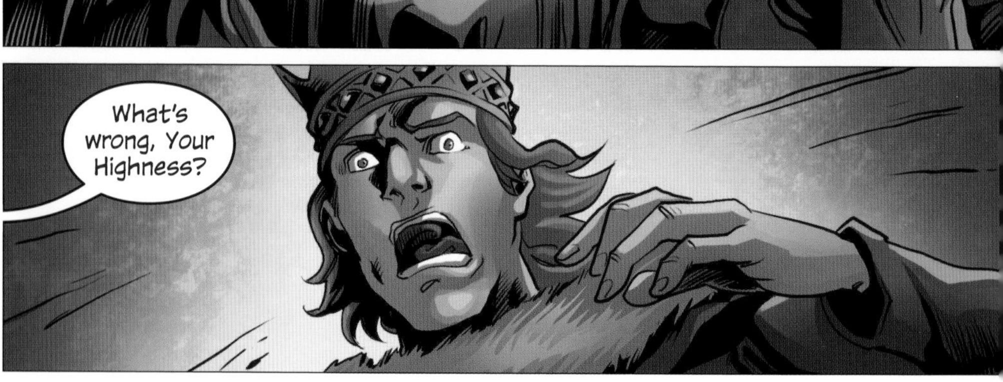
What's wrong, Your Highness?

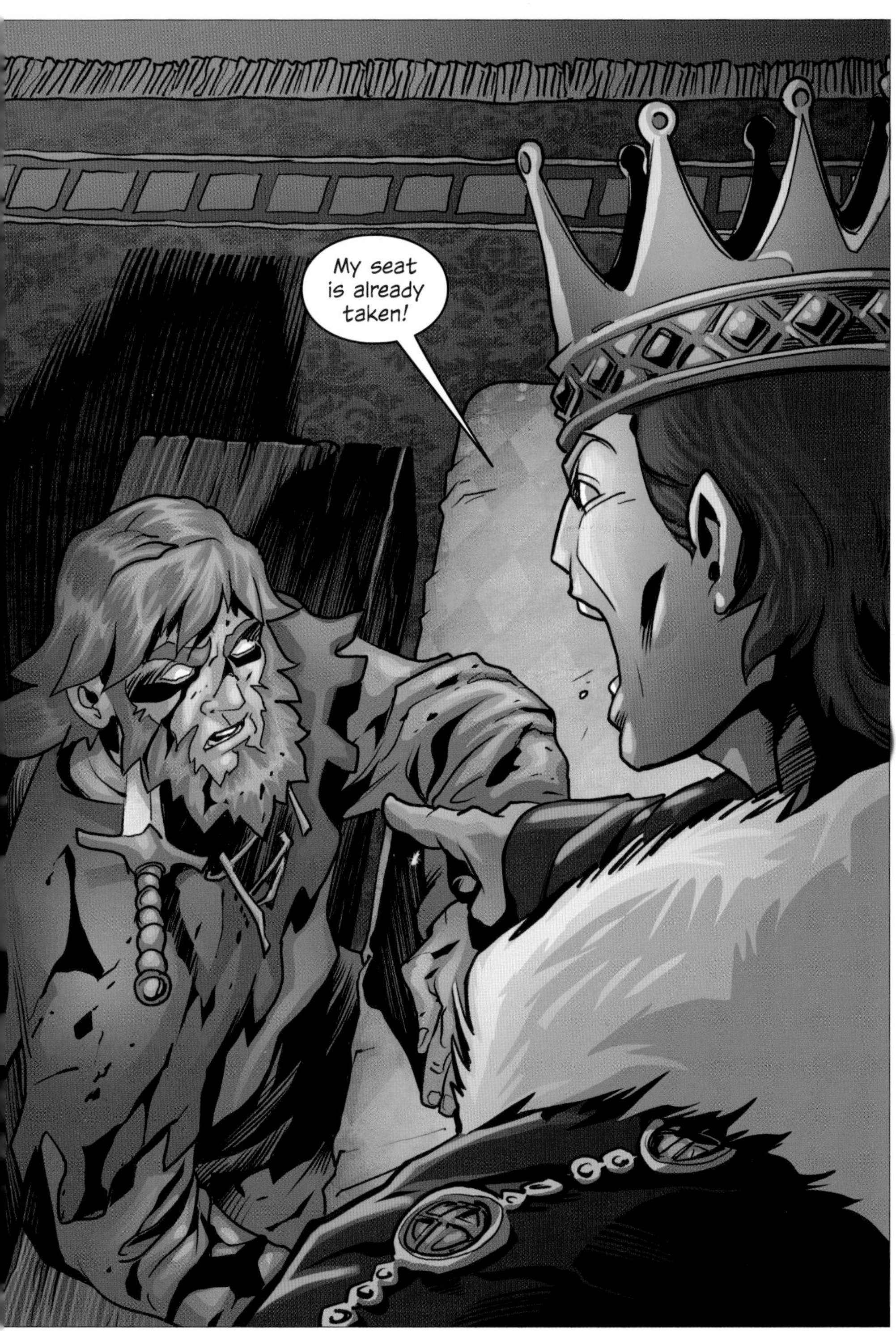
My seat is already taken!

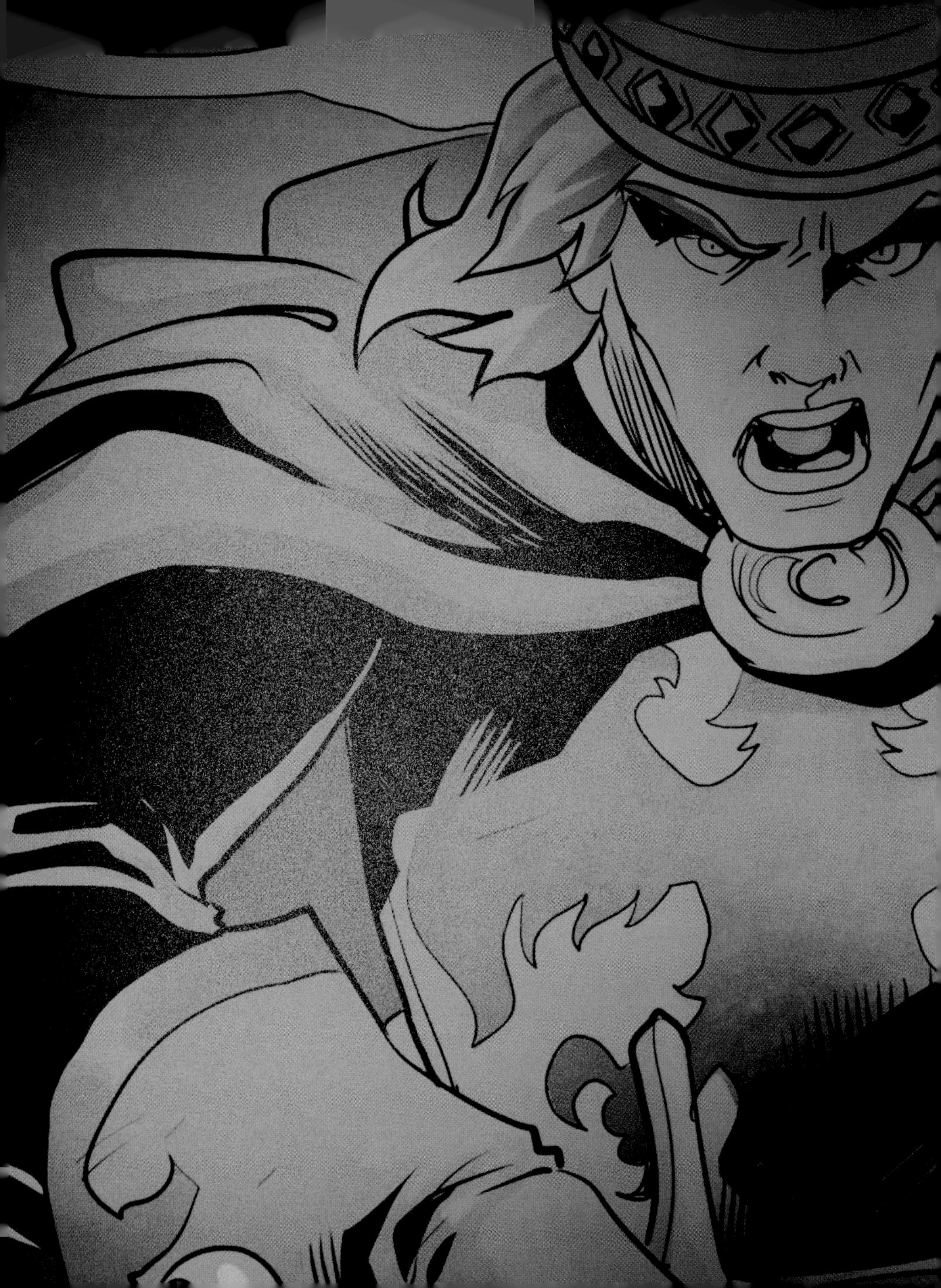

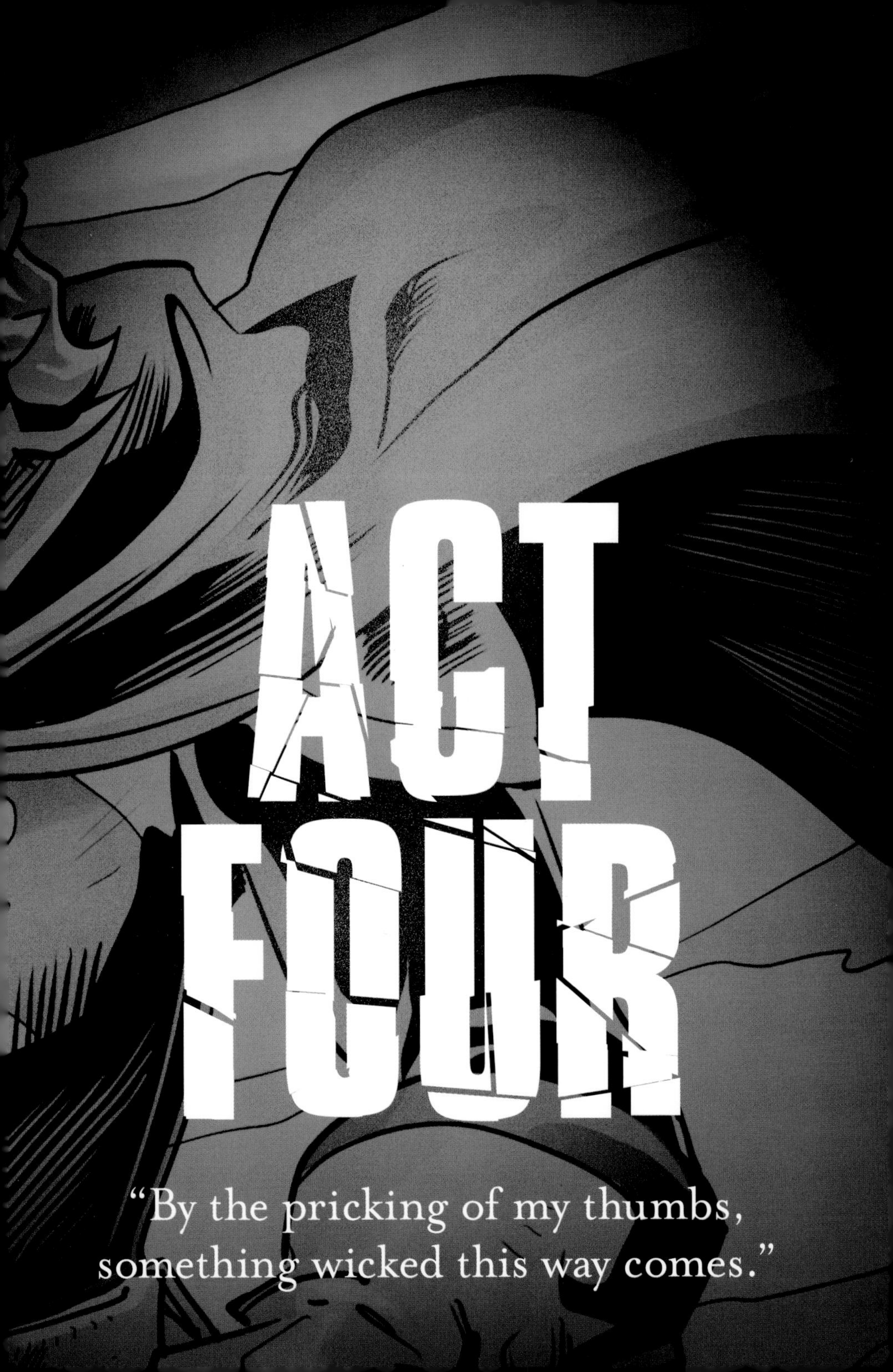

ACT FOUR

"By the pricking of my thumbs,
something wicked this way comes."

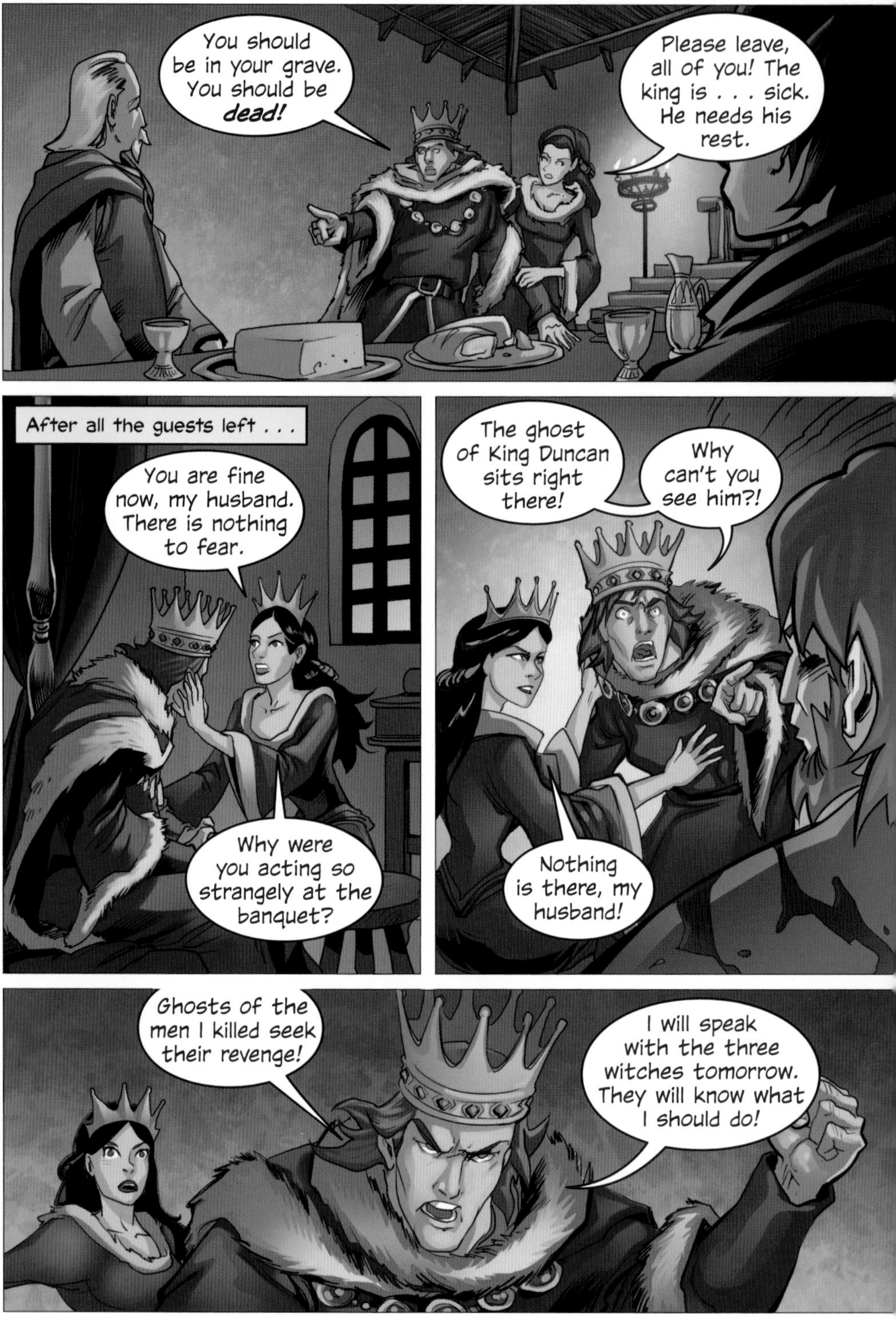
You should be in your grave. You should be *dead!*
Please leave, all of you! The king is . . . sick. He needs his rest.
After all the guests left . . .
You are fine now, my husband. There is nothing to fear.
Why were you acting so strangely at the banquet?
The ghost of King Duncan sits right there!
Why can't you see him?!
Nothing is there, my husband!
Ghosts of the men I killed seek their revenge!
I will speak with the three witches tomorrow. They will know what I should do!

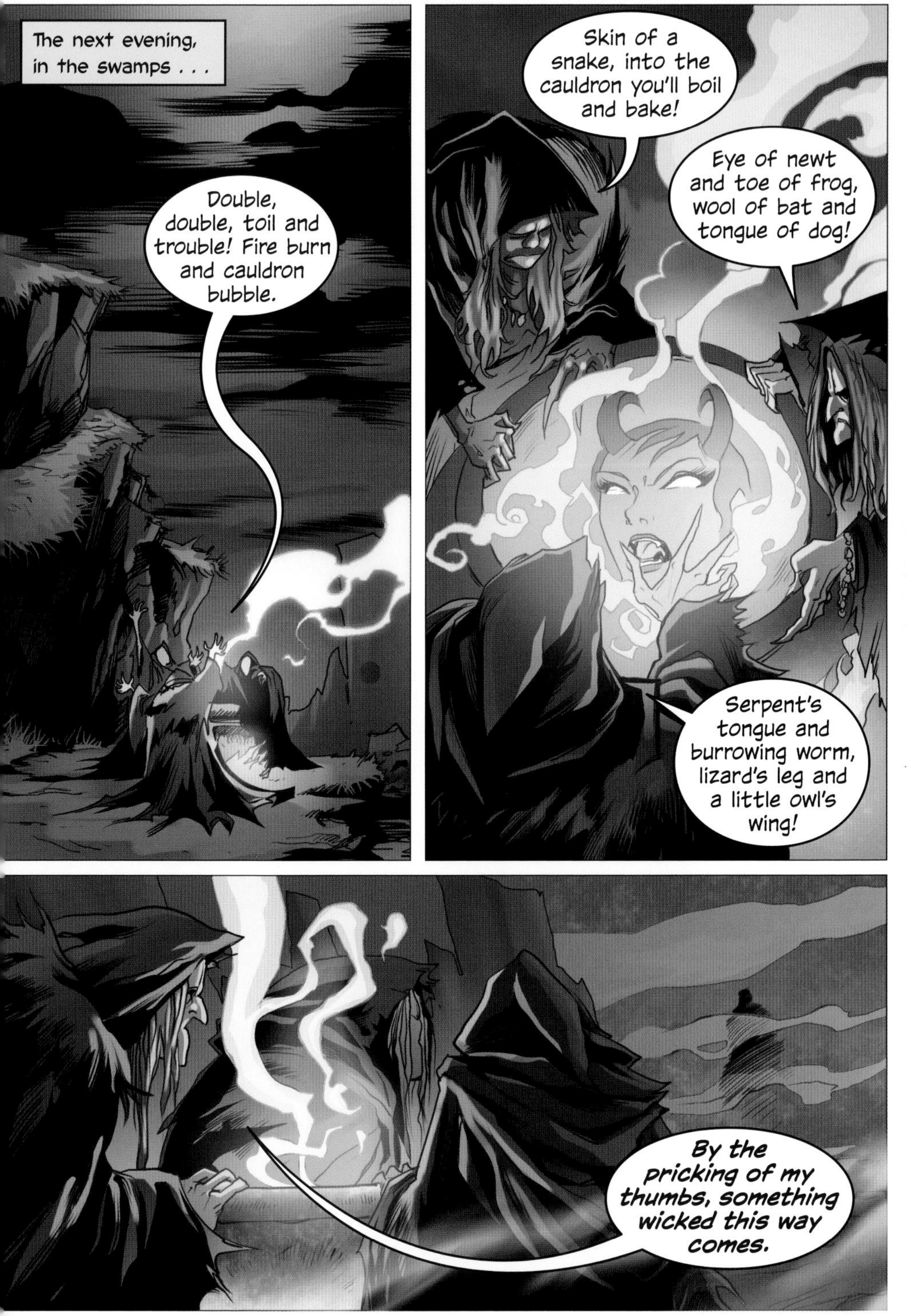
The next evening, in the swamps . . .
Double, double, toil and trouble! Fire burn and cauldron bubble.
Skin of a snake, into the cauldron you'll boil and bake!
Eye of newt and toe of frog, wool of bat and tongue of dog!
Serpent's tongue and burrowing worm, lizard's leg and a little owl's wing!
By the pricking of my thumbs, something wicked this way comes.

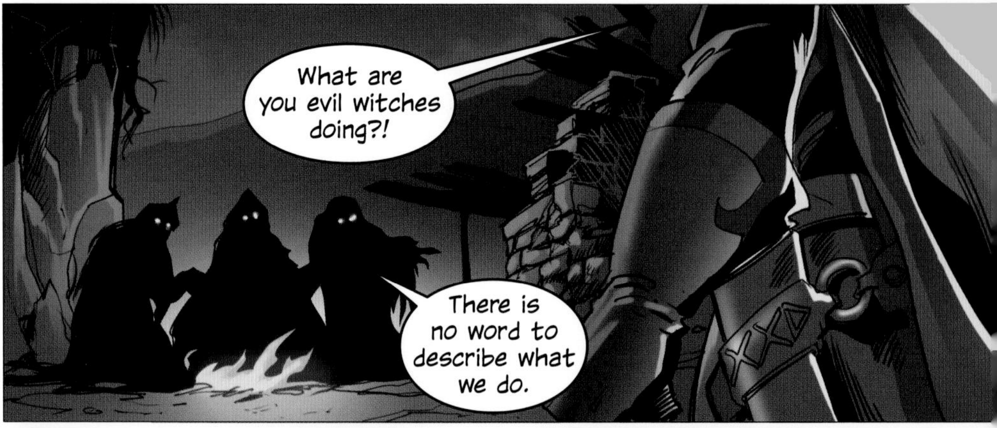
What are you evil witches doing?!
There is no word to describe what we do.

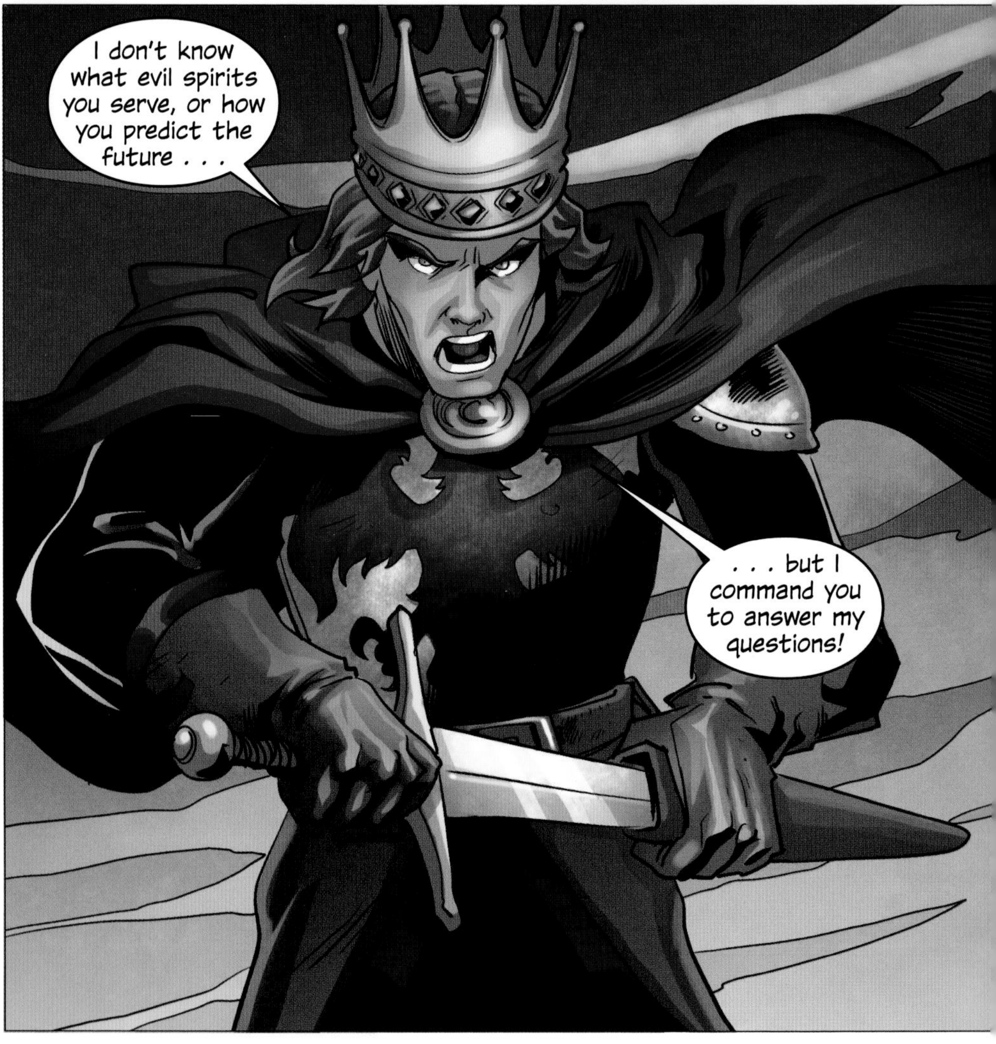
I don't know what evil spirits you serve, or how you predict the future . . .
. . . but I command you to answer my questions!

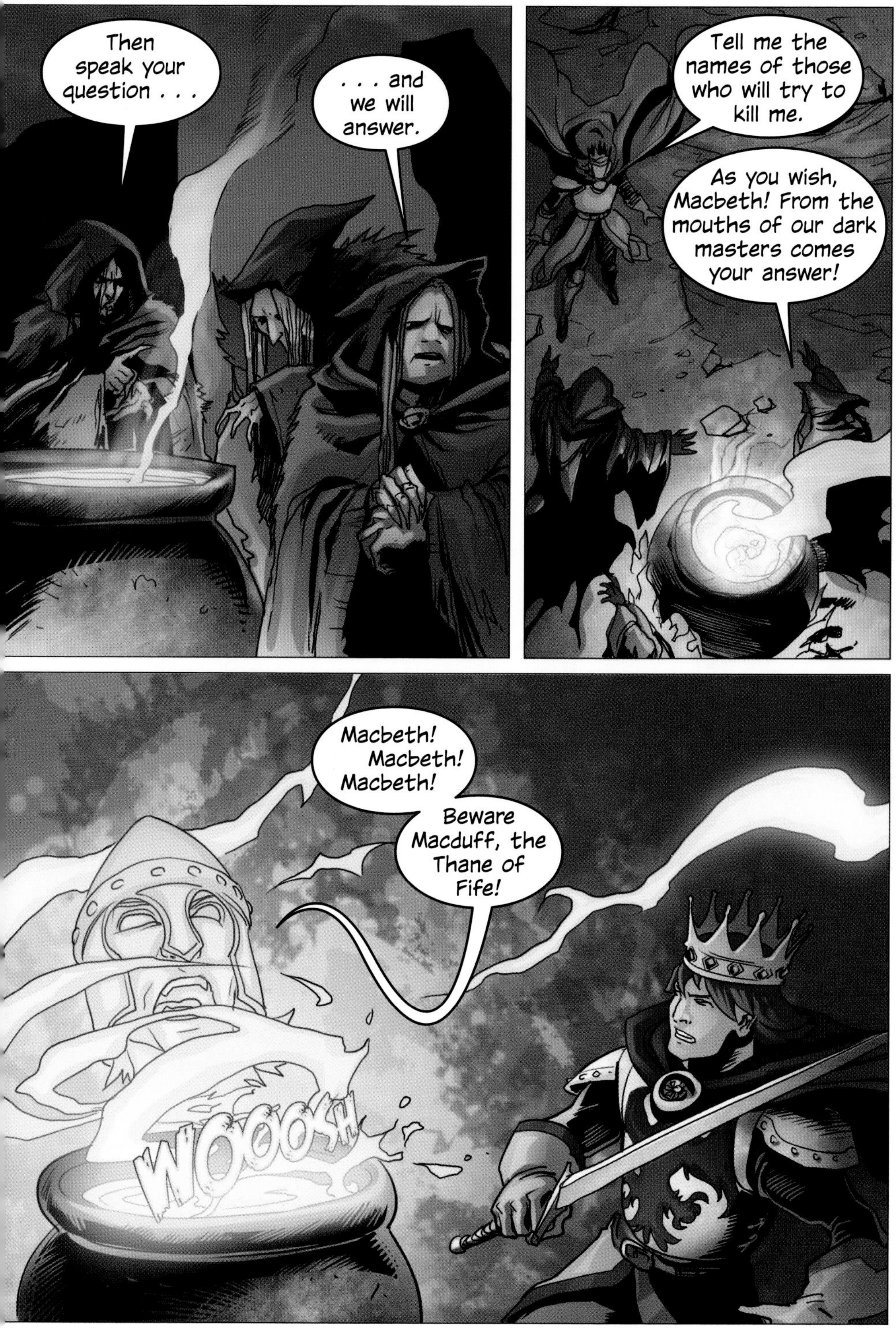
Then speak your question . . .
. . . and we will answer.
Tell me the names of those who will try to kill me.
As you wish, Macbeth! From the mouths of our dark masters comes your answer!
Macbeth! Macbeth! Macbeth!
Beware Macduff, the Thane of Fife!
WOOOSH

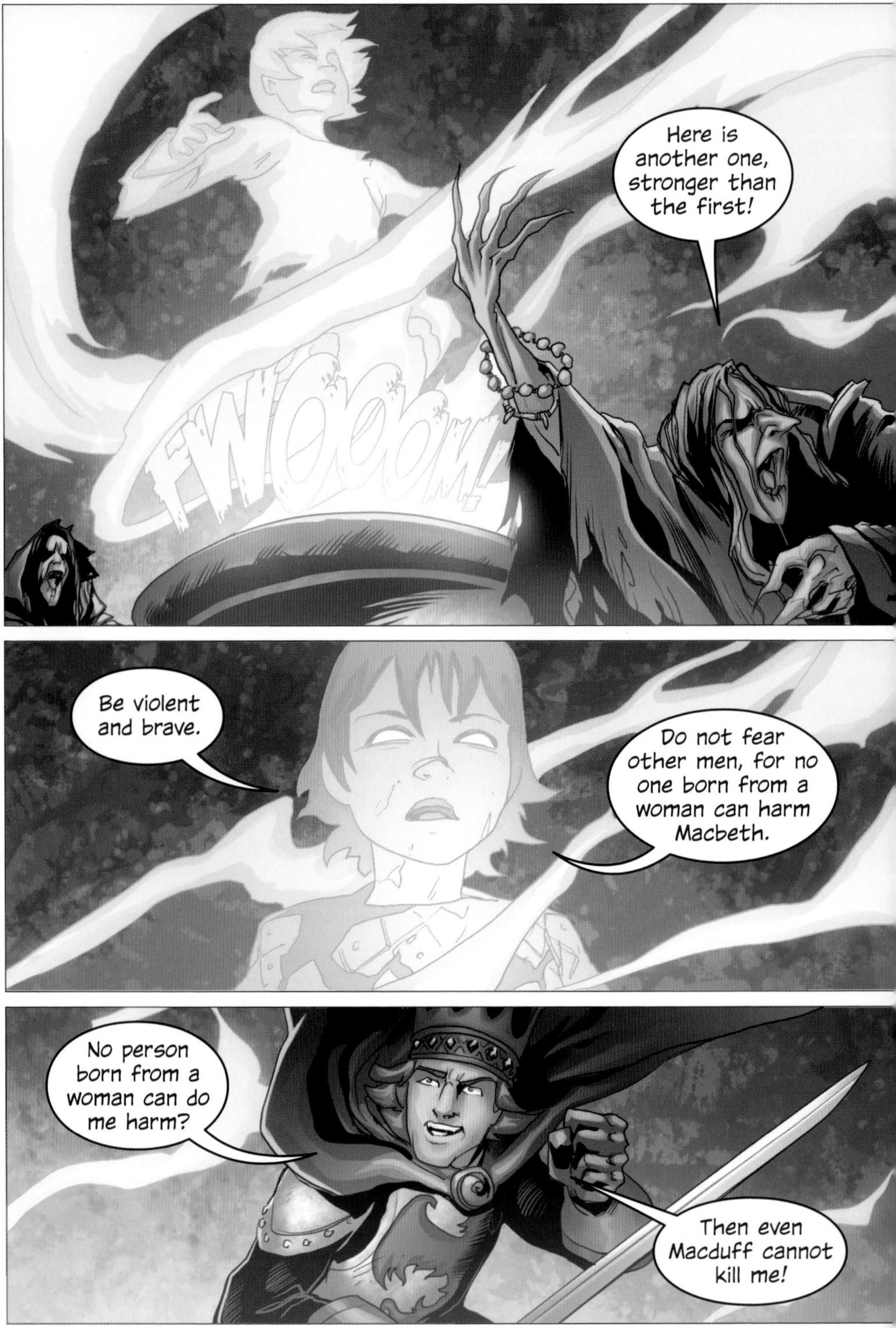
Here is another one, stronger than the first!
FWOOOM!
Be violent and brave.
Do not fear other men, for no one born from a woman can harm Macbeth.
No person born from a woman can do me harm?
Then even Macduff cannot kill me!

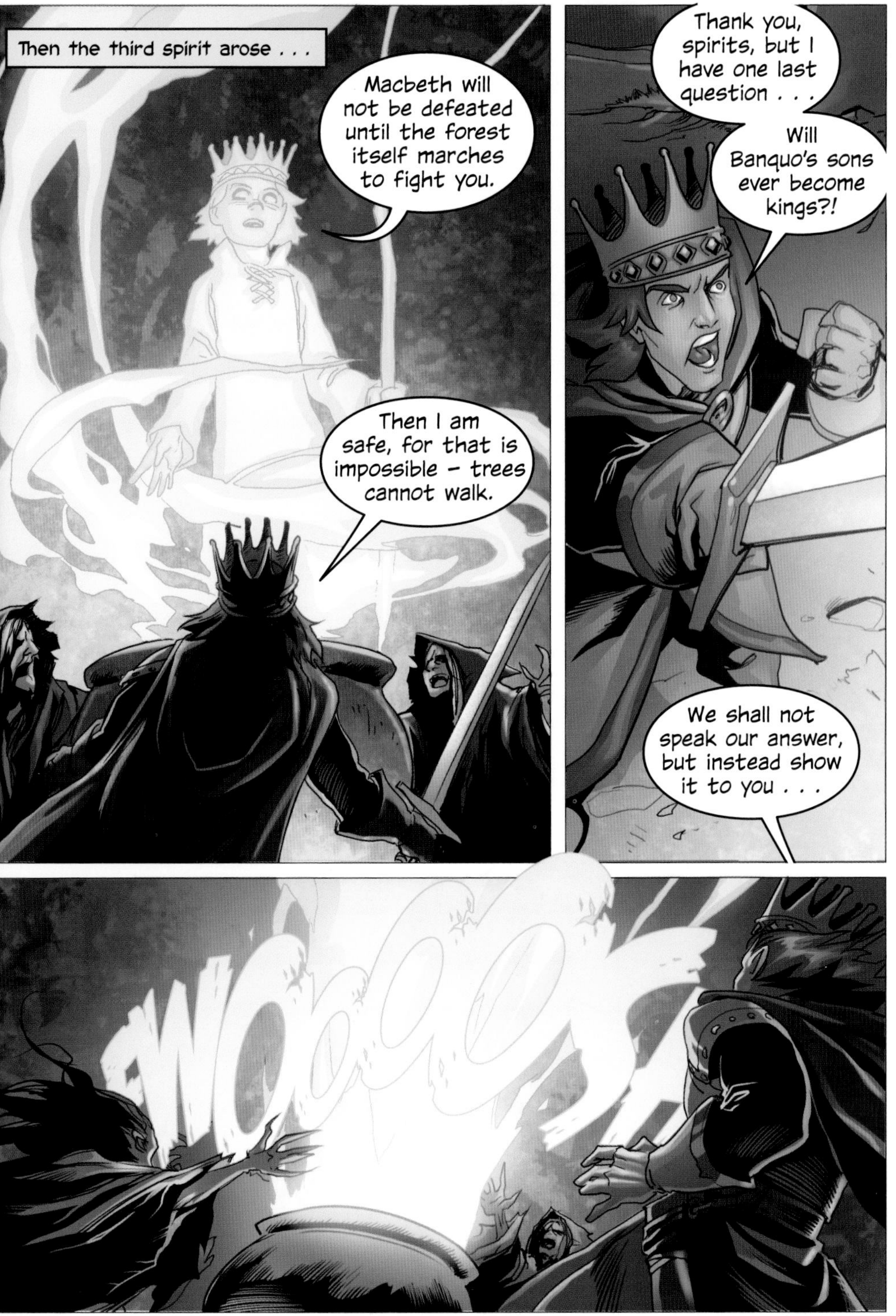
Then the third spirit arose . . .
Macbeth will not be defeated until the forest itself marches to fight you.
Then I am safe, for that is impossible - trees cannot walk.
Thank you, spirits, but I have one last question . . .
Will Banquo's sons ever become kings?!
We shall not speak our answer, but instead show it to you . . .

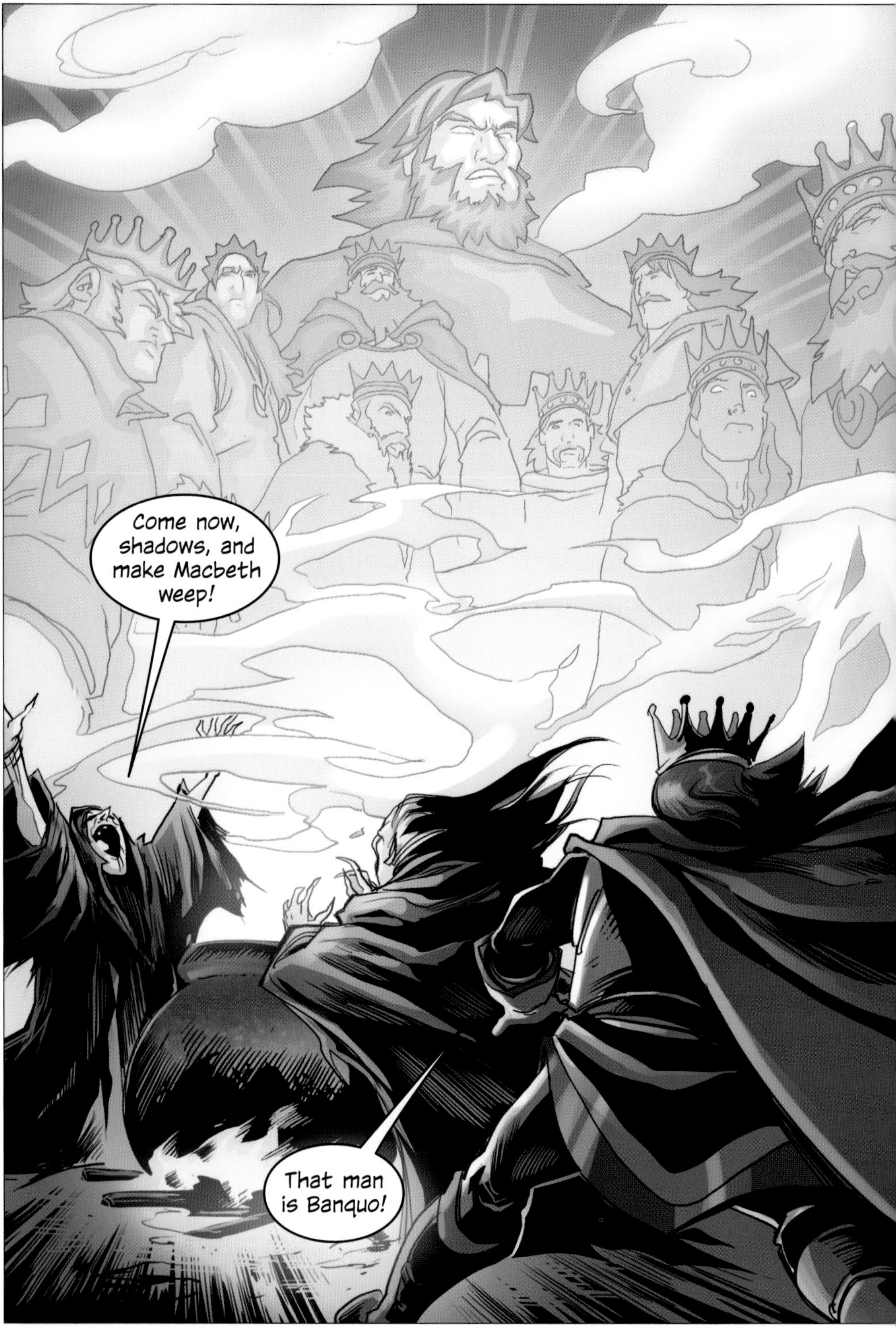
Come now, shadows, and make Macbeth weep!
That man is Banquo!

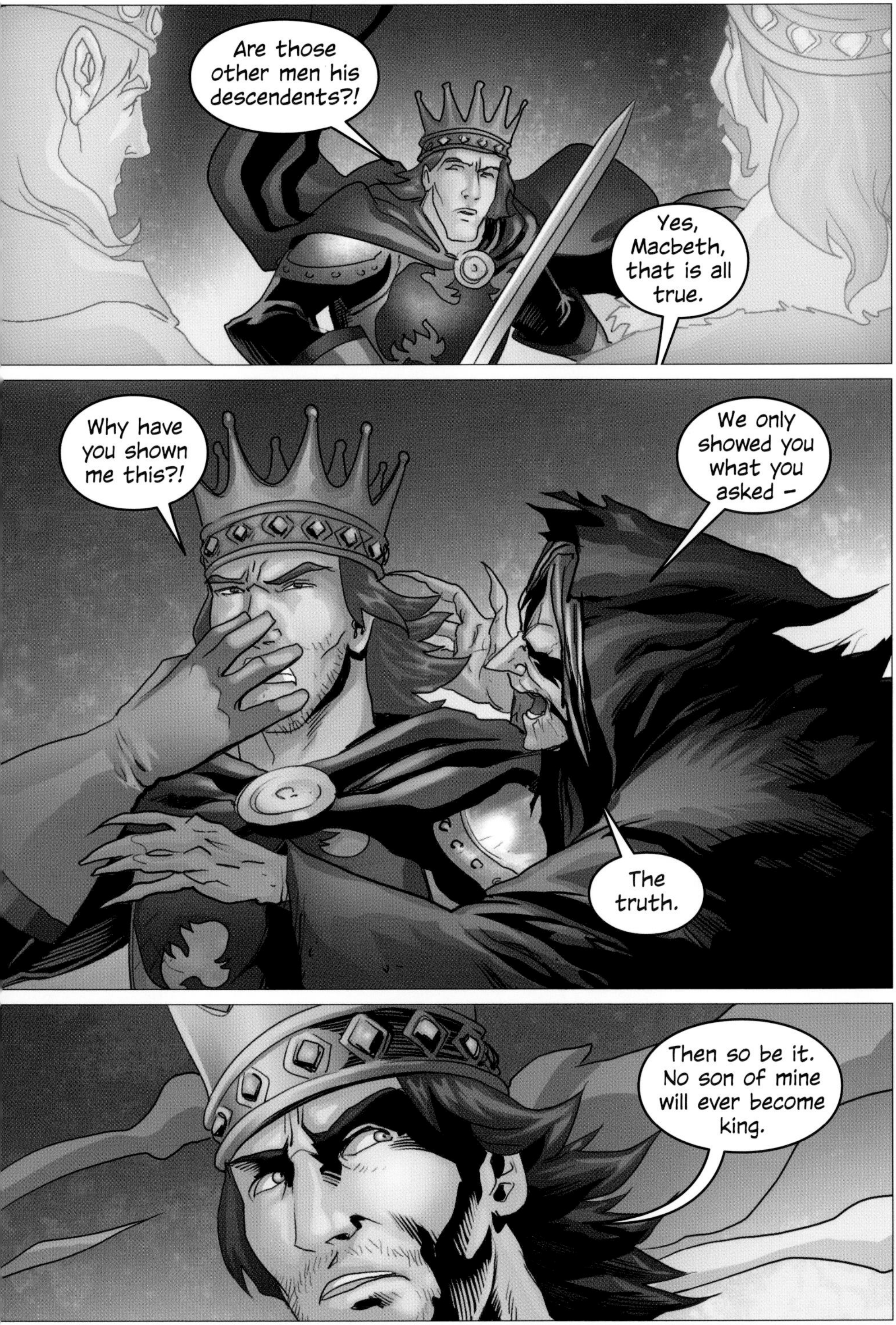
Are those other men his descendents?!
Yes, Macbeth, that is all true.
Why have you shown me this?!
We only showed you what you asked –
The truth.
Then so be it. No son of mine will ever become king.

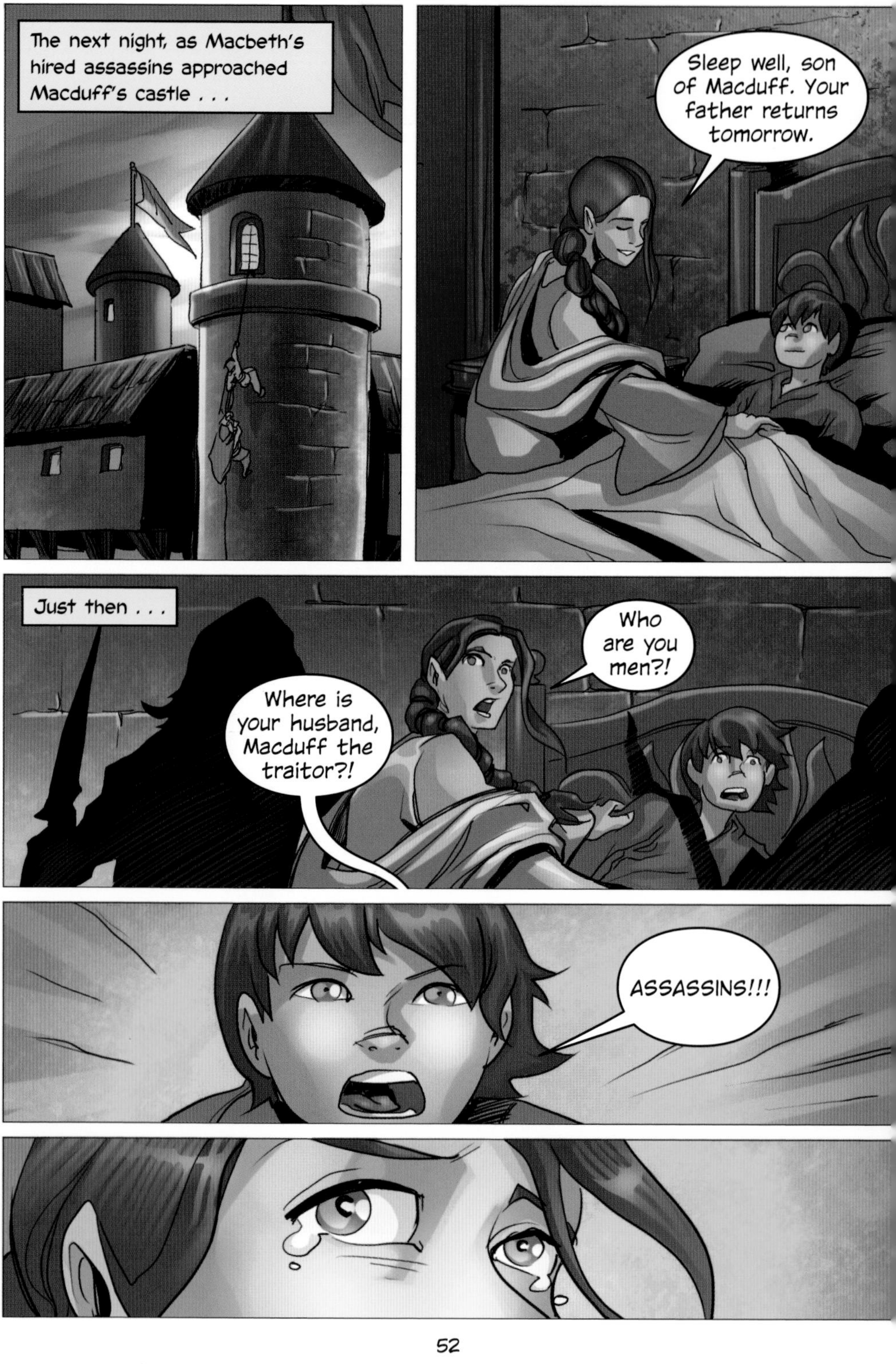
The next night, as Macbeth's hired assassins approached Macduff's castle . . .
Sleep well, son of Macduff. Your father returns tomorrow.
Just then . . .
Who are you men?!
Where is your husband, Macduff the traitor?!
ASSASSINS!!!

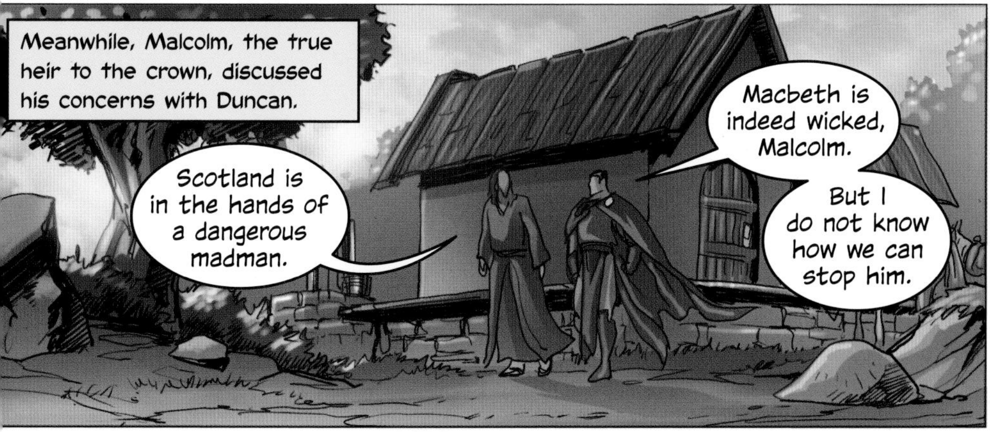
Meanwhile, Malcolm, the true heir to the crown, discussed his concerns with Duncan.
Scotland is in the hands of a dangerous madman.
Macbeth is indeed wicked, Malcolm.
But I do not know how we can stop him.

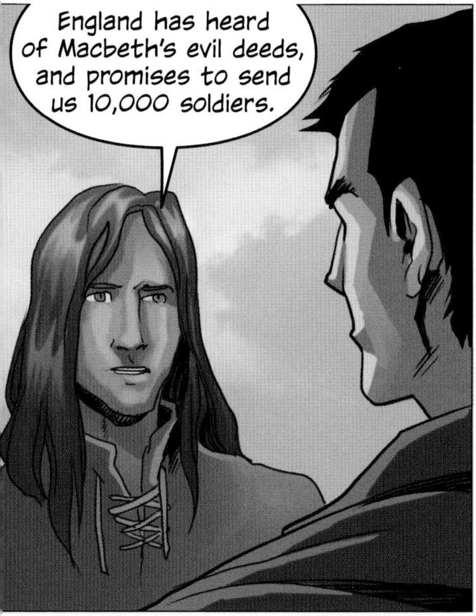
England has heard of Macbeth's evil deeds, and promises to send us 10,000 soldiers.

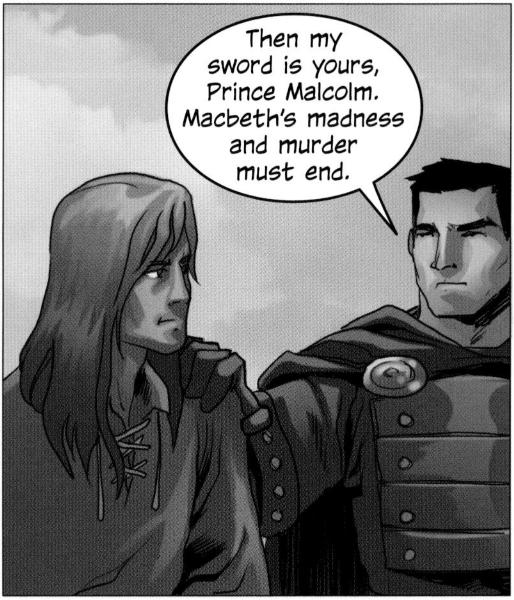
Then my sword is yours, Prince Malcolm. Macbeth's madness and murder must end.

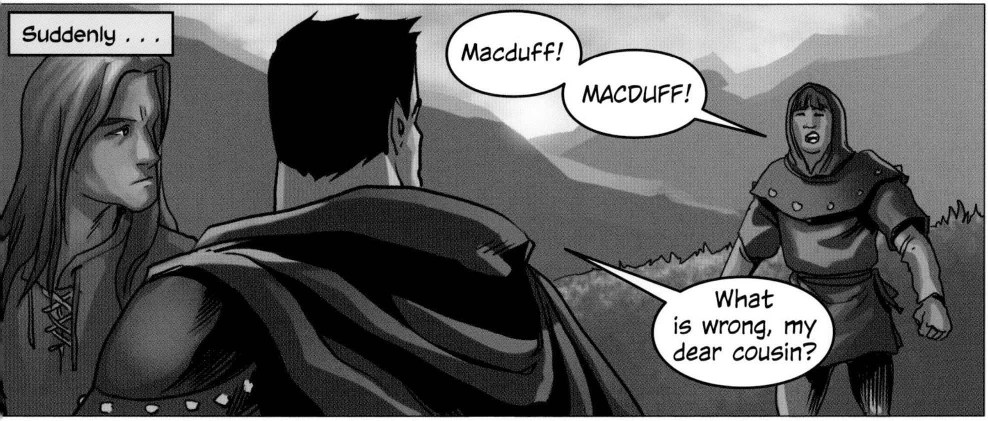
Suddenly . . .
Macduff!
MACDUFF!
What is wrong, my dear cousin?

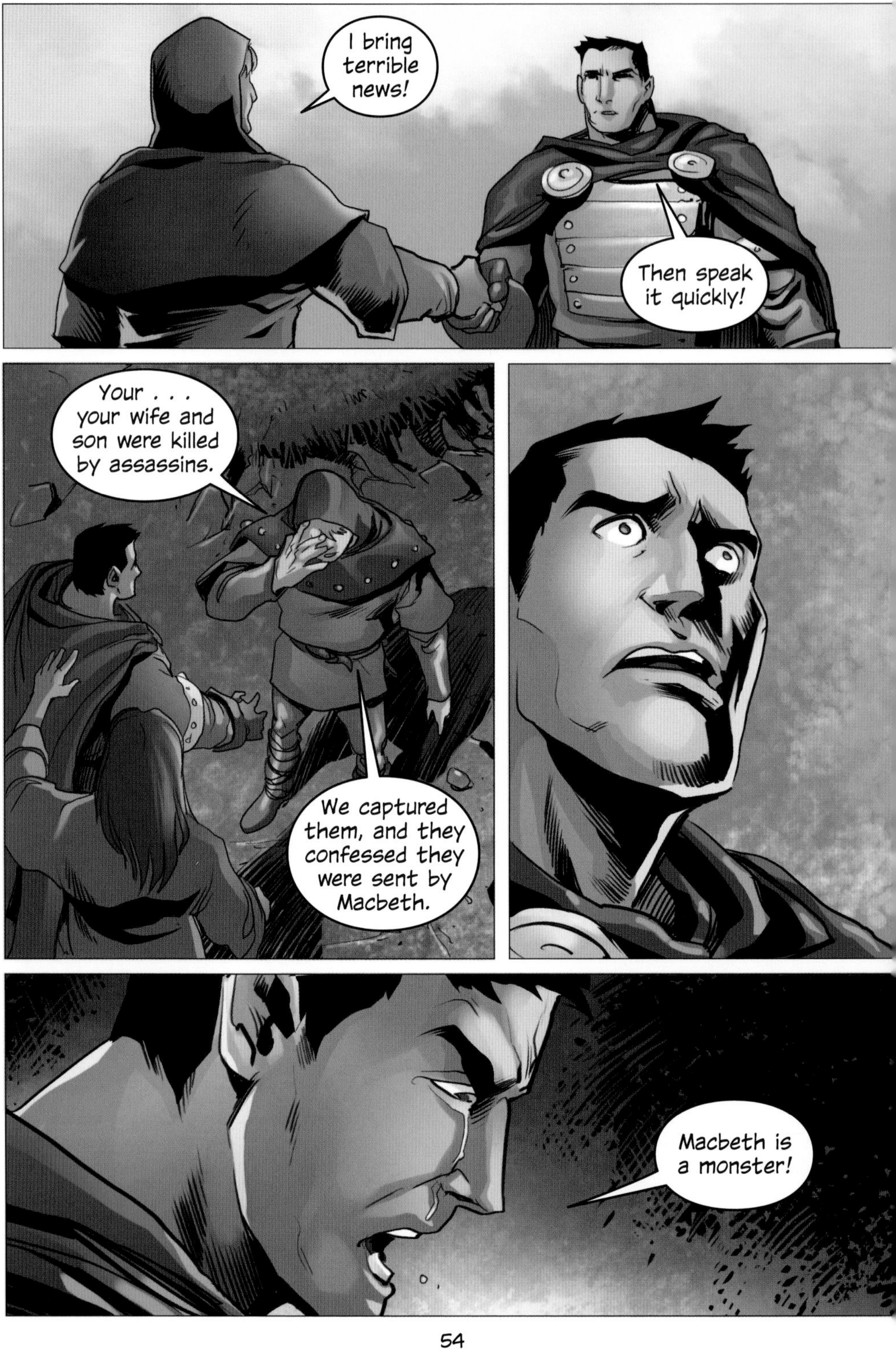
I bring terrible news!
Then speak it quickly!
Your . . . your wife and son were killed by assassins.
We captured them, and they confessed they were sent by Macbeth.
Macbeth is a monster!

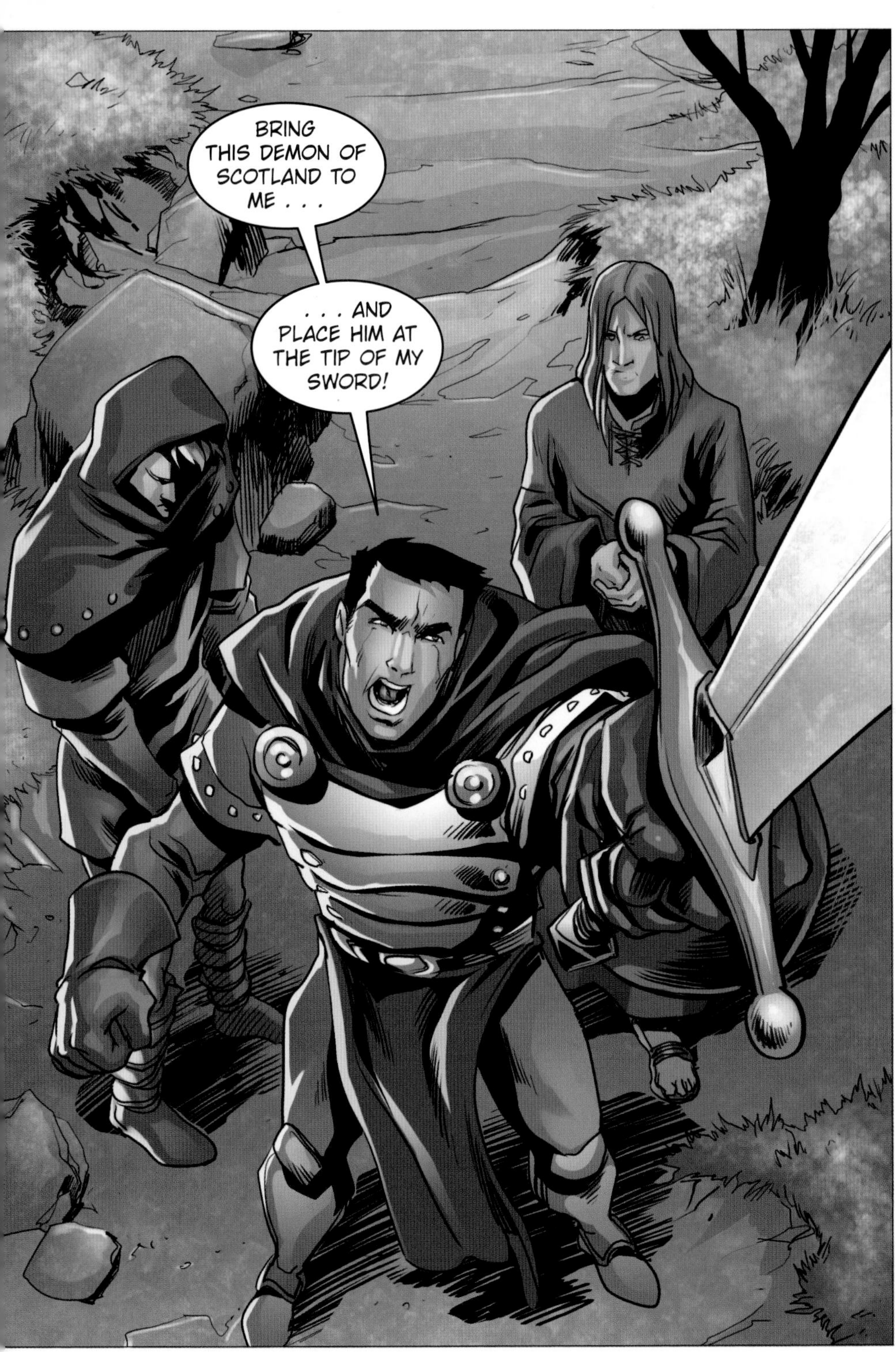
BRING THIS DEMON OF SCOTLAND TO ME . . .
. . . AND PLACE HIM AT THE TIP OF MY SWORD!

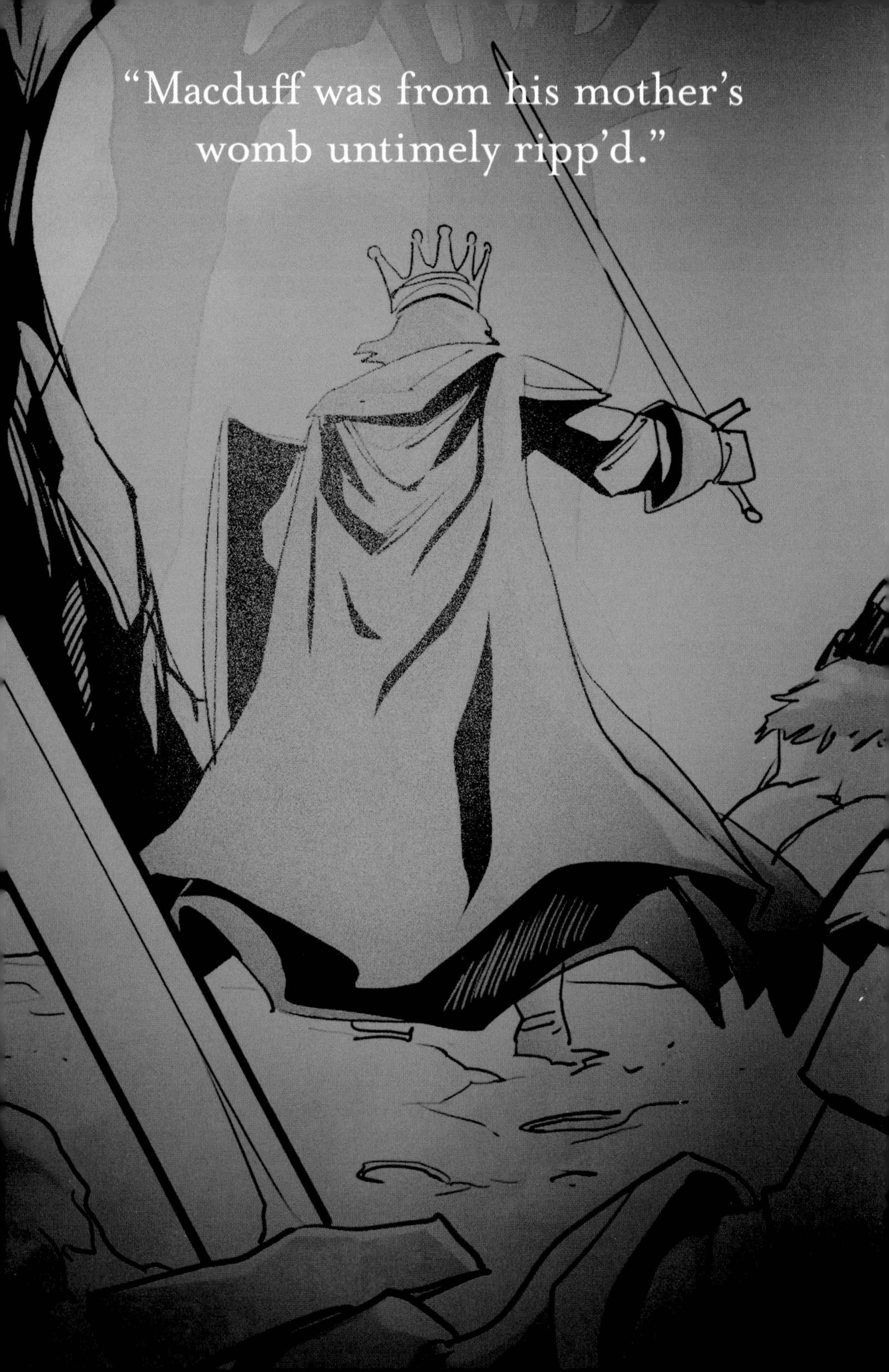
"Macduff was from his mother's womb untimely ripp'd."

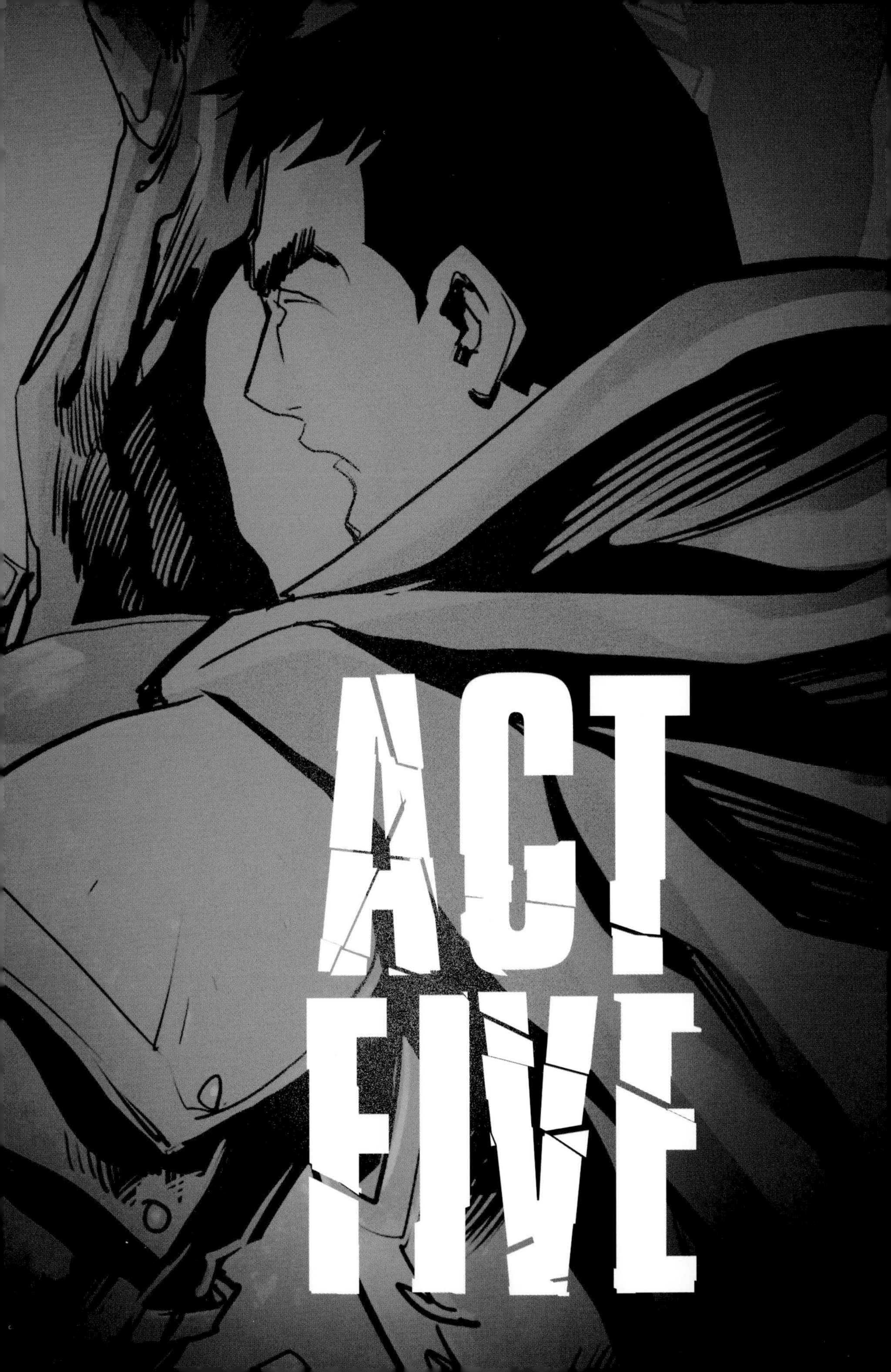
ACT
FIVE

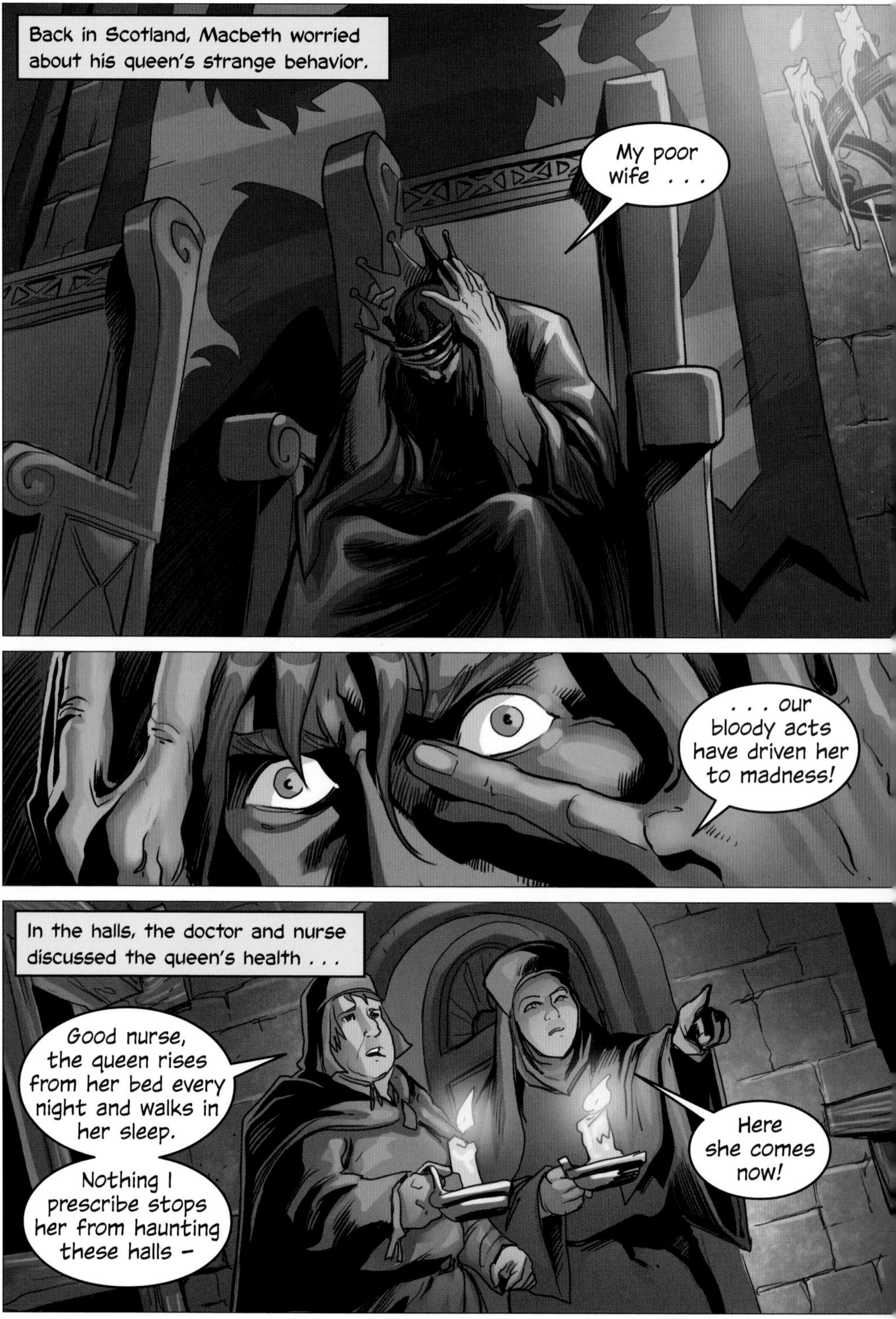
Back in Scotland, Macbeth worried about his queen's strange behavior.
My poor wife . . .
. . . our bloody acts have driven her to madness!
In the halls, the doctor and nurse discussed the queen's health . . .
Good nurse, the queen rises from her bed every night and walks in her sleep.
Nothing I prescribe stops her from haunting these halls –
Here she comes now!

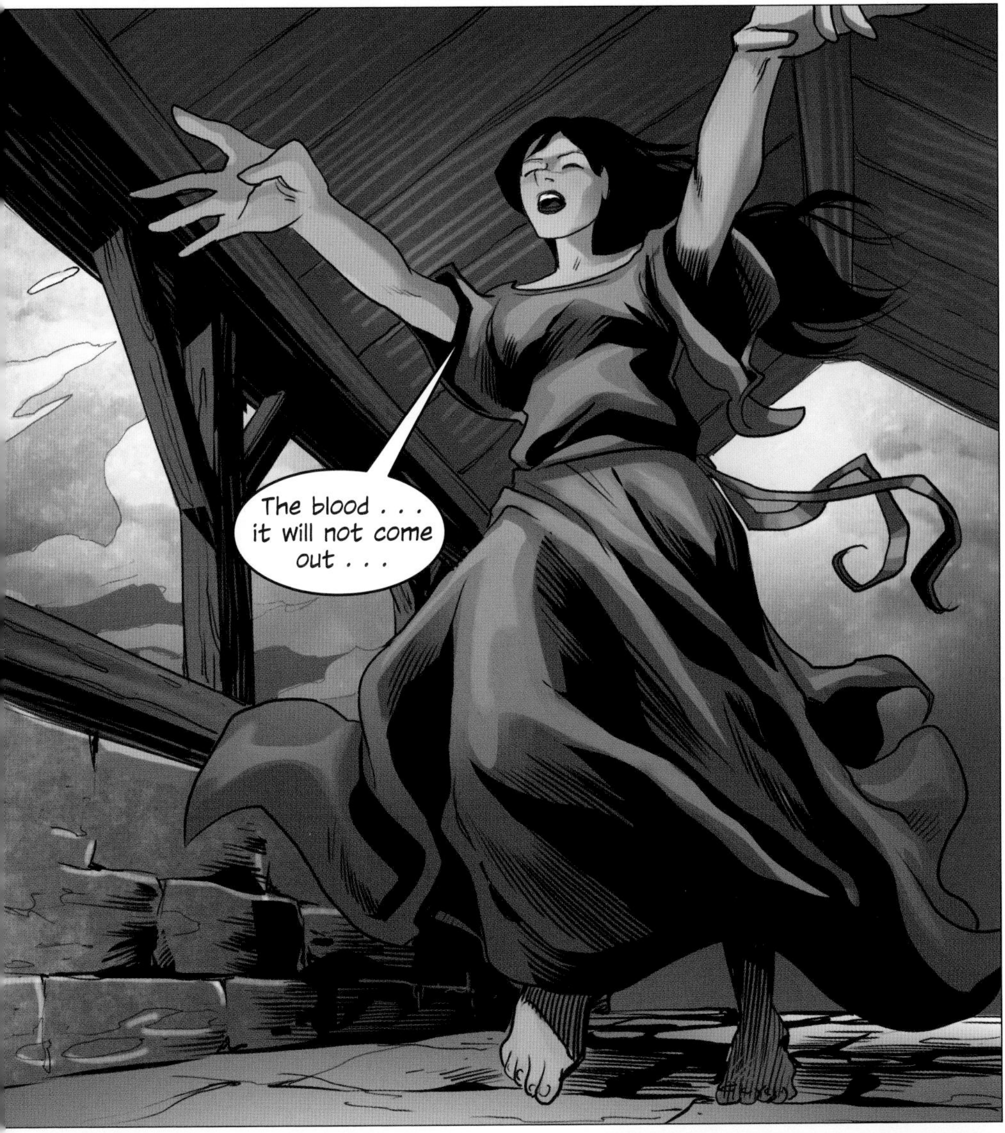
The blood . . . it will not come out . . .

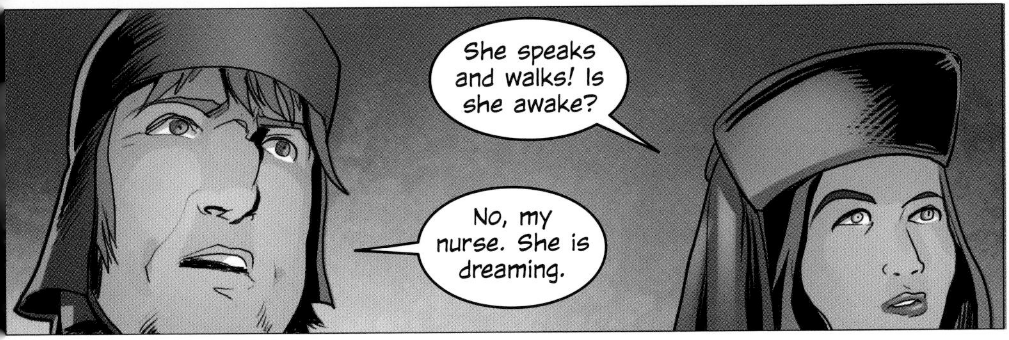
She speaks and walks! Is she awake?
No, my nurse. She is dreaming.

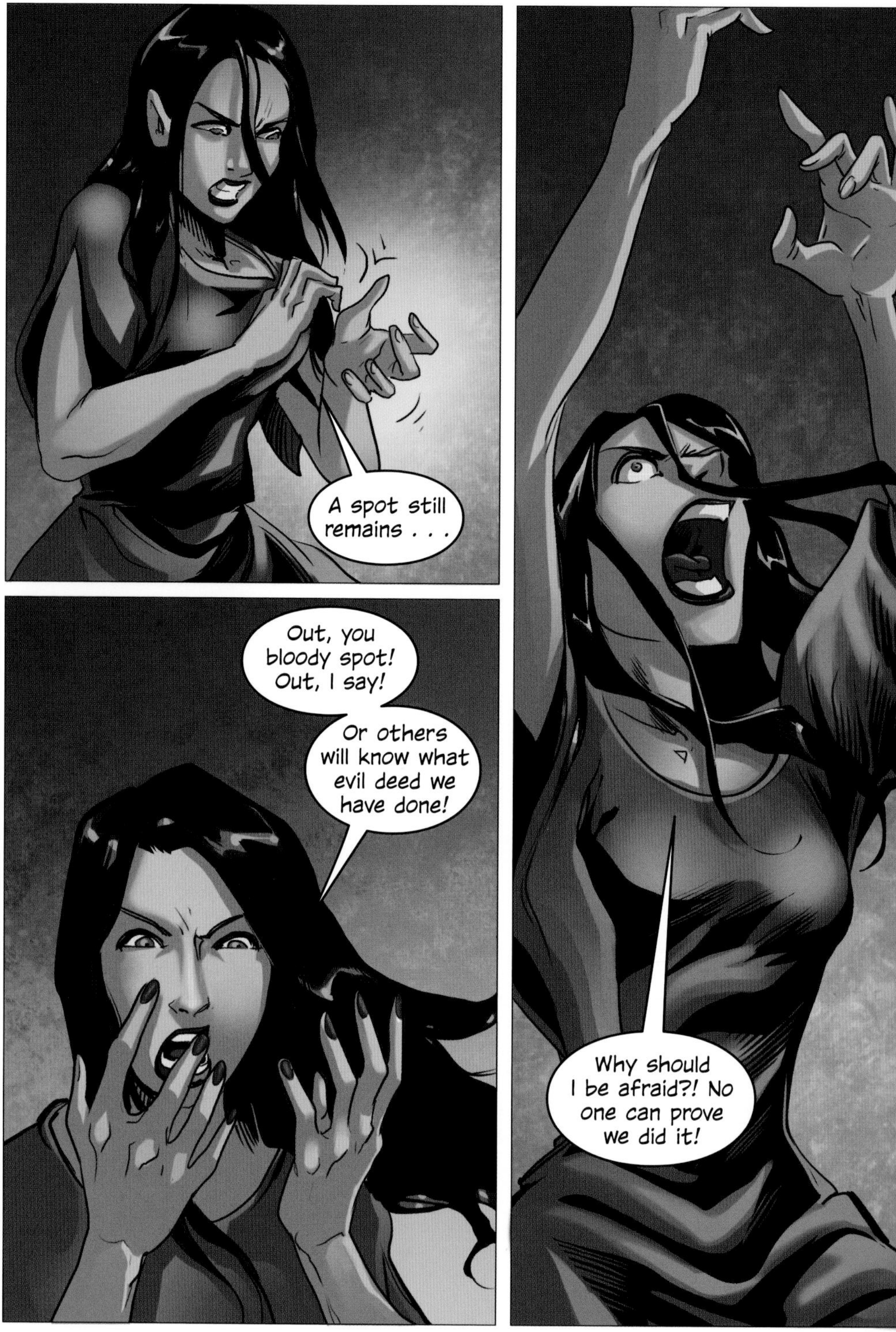
A spot still remains . . .
Out, you bloody spot! Out, I say!
Or others will know what evil deed we have done!
Why should I be afraid?! No one can prove we did it!

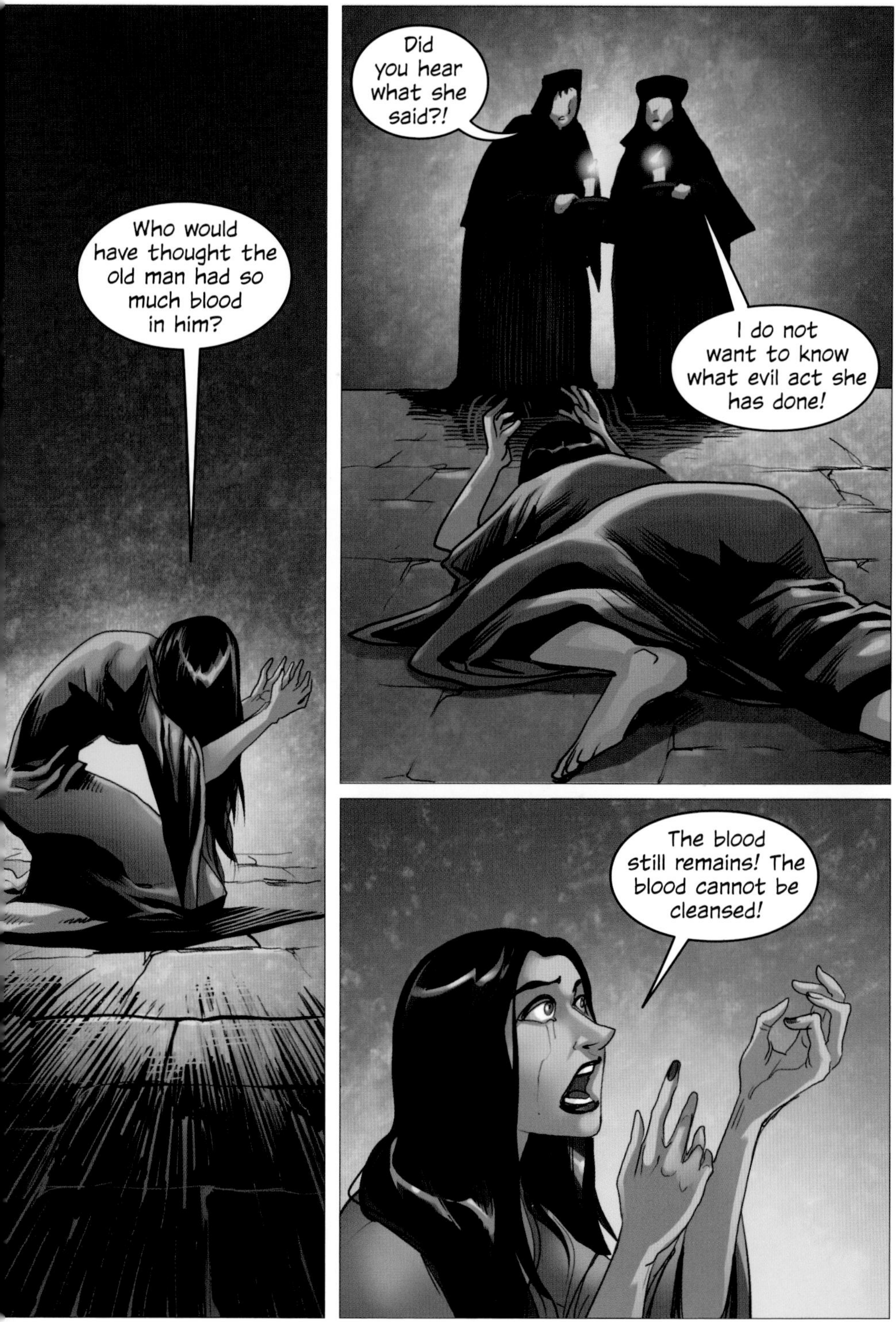
Who would have thought the old man had so much blood in him?
Did you hear what she said?!
I do not want to know what evil act she has done!
The blood still remains! The blood cannot be cleansed!

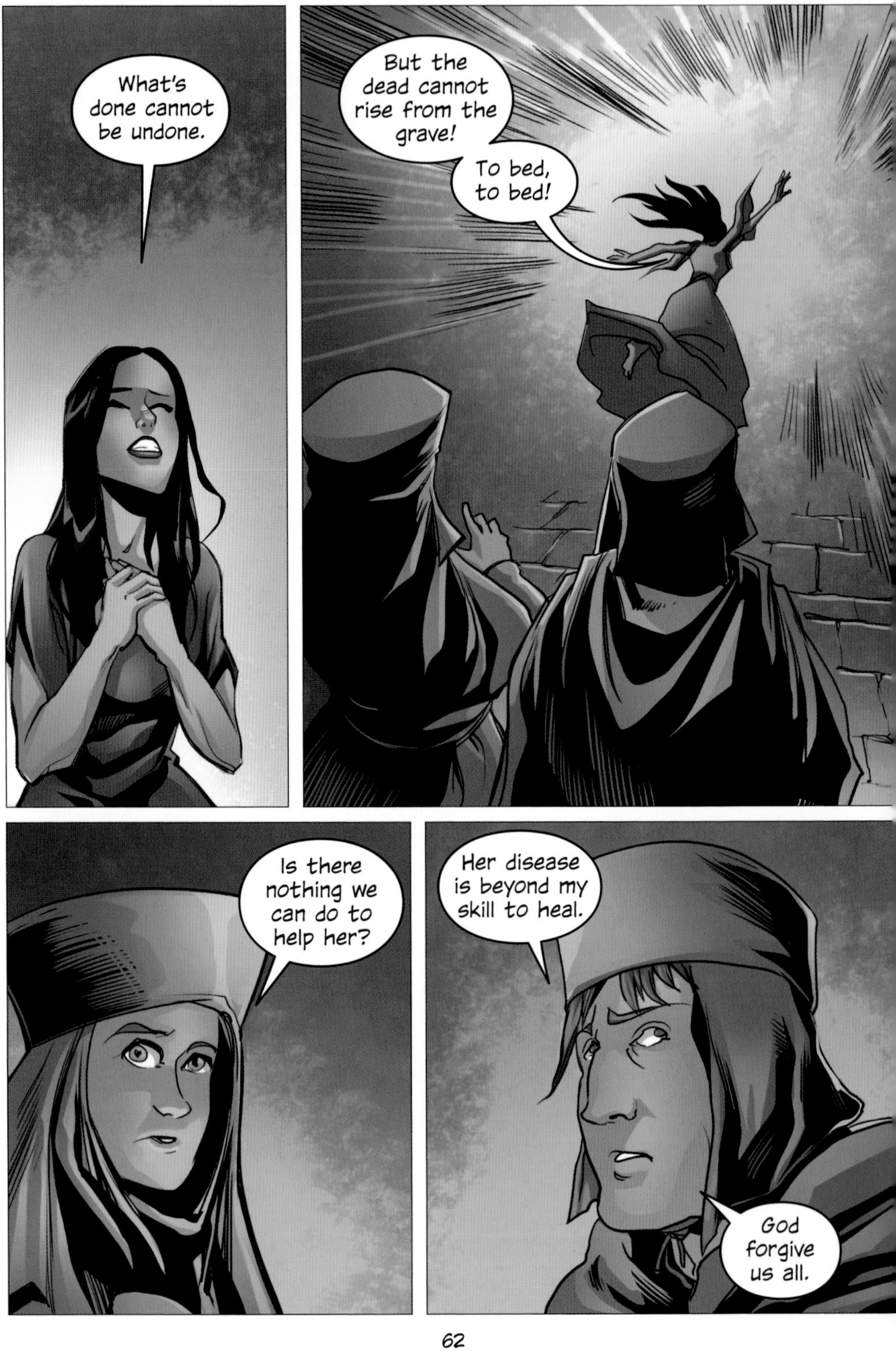
What's done cannot be undone.
But the dead cannot rise from the grave!
To bed, to bed!
Is there nothing we can do to help her?
Her disease is beyond my skill to heal.
God forgive us all.

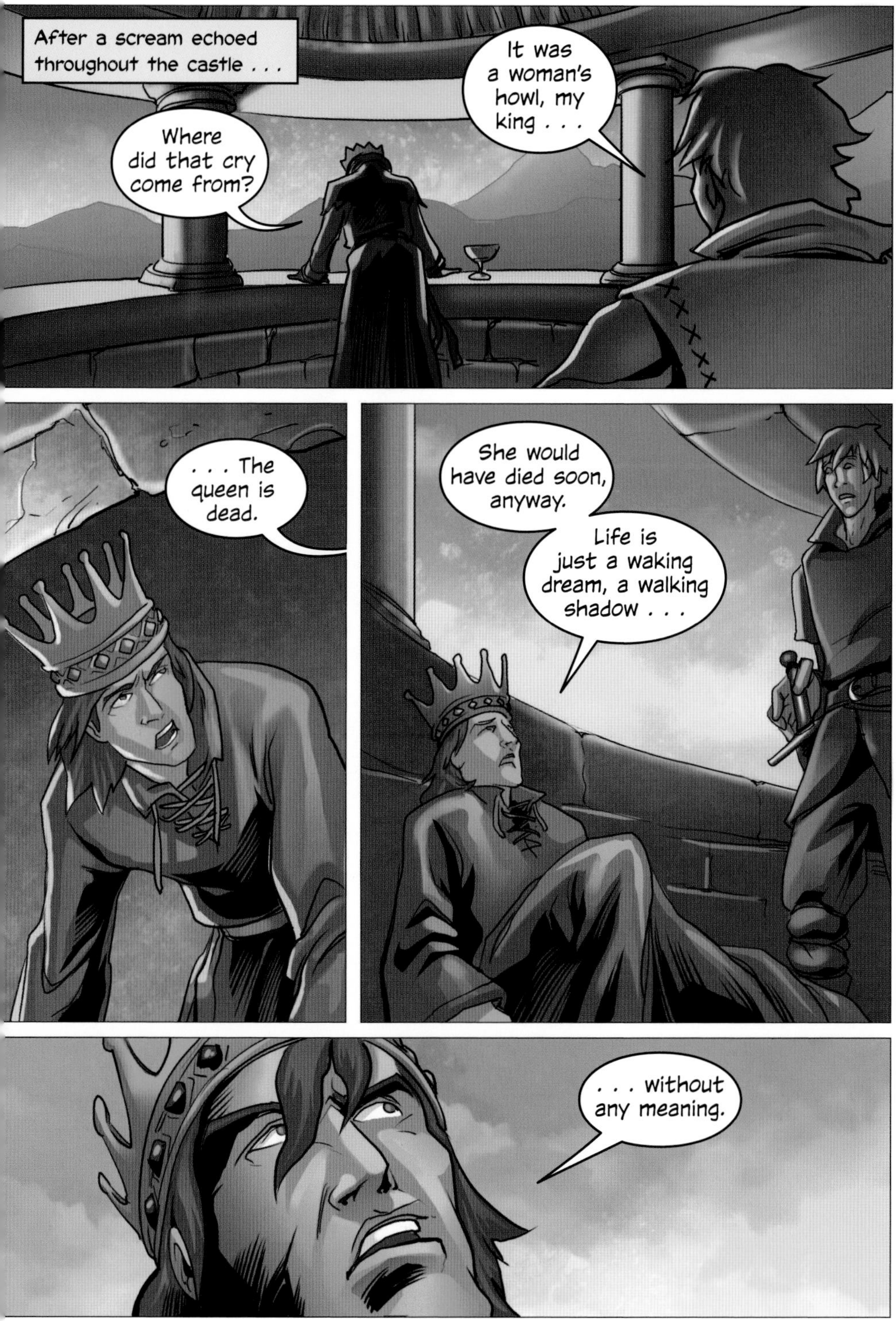
After a scream echoed throughout the castle . . .
Where did that cry come from?
It was a woman's howl, my king . . .
. . . The queen is dead.
She would have died soon, anyway.
Life is just a waking dream, a walking shadow . . .
. . . without any meaning.

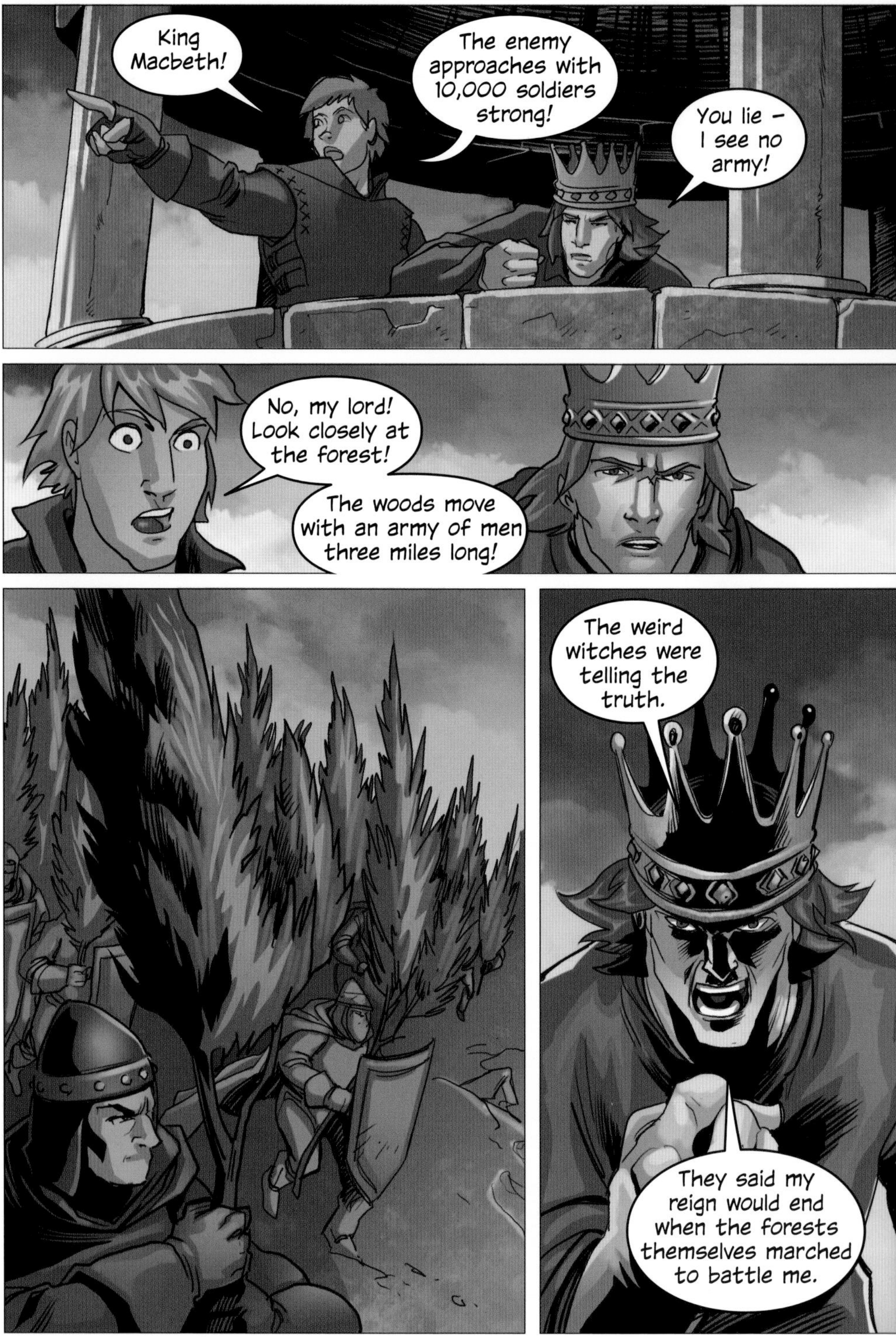
King Macbeth!
The enemy approaches with 10,000 soldiers strong!
You lie – I see no army!
No, my lord! Look closely at the forest!
The woods move with an army of men three miles long!
The weird witches were telling the truth.
They said my reign would end when the forests themselves marched to battle me.

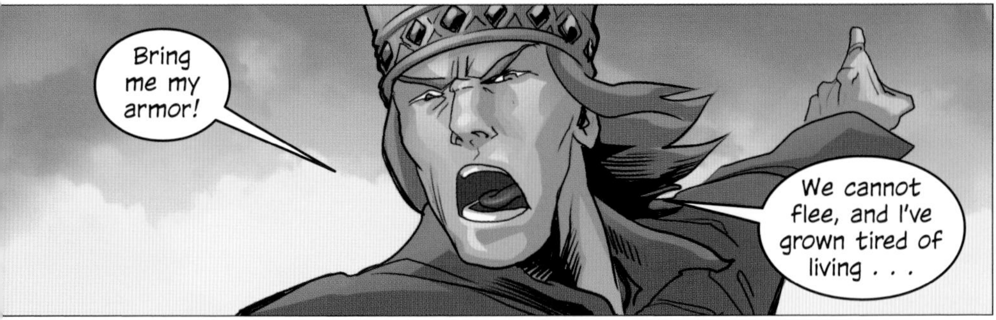
Bring me my armor!
We cannot flee, and I've grown tired of living . . .

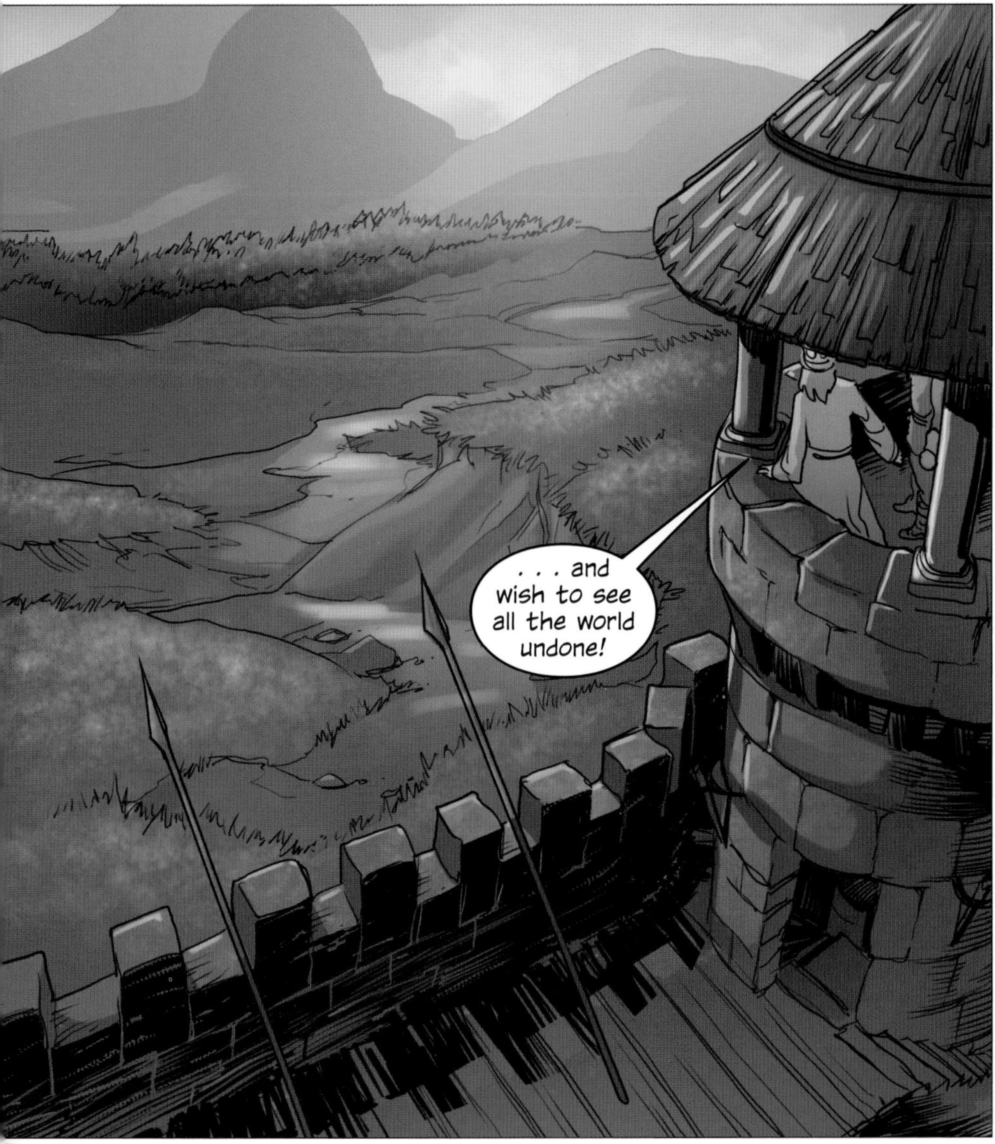
. . . and wish to see all the world undone!

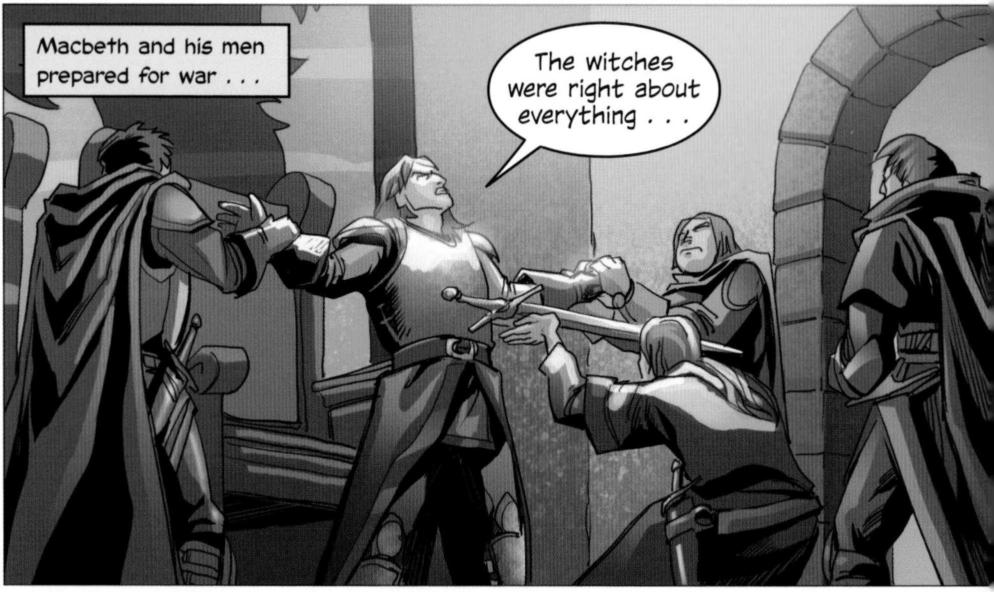
Macbeth and his men prepared for war . . .
The witches were right about everything . . .

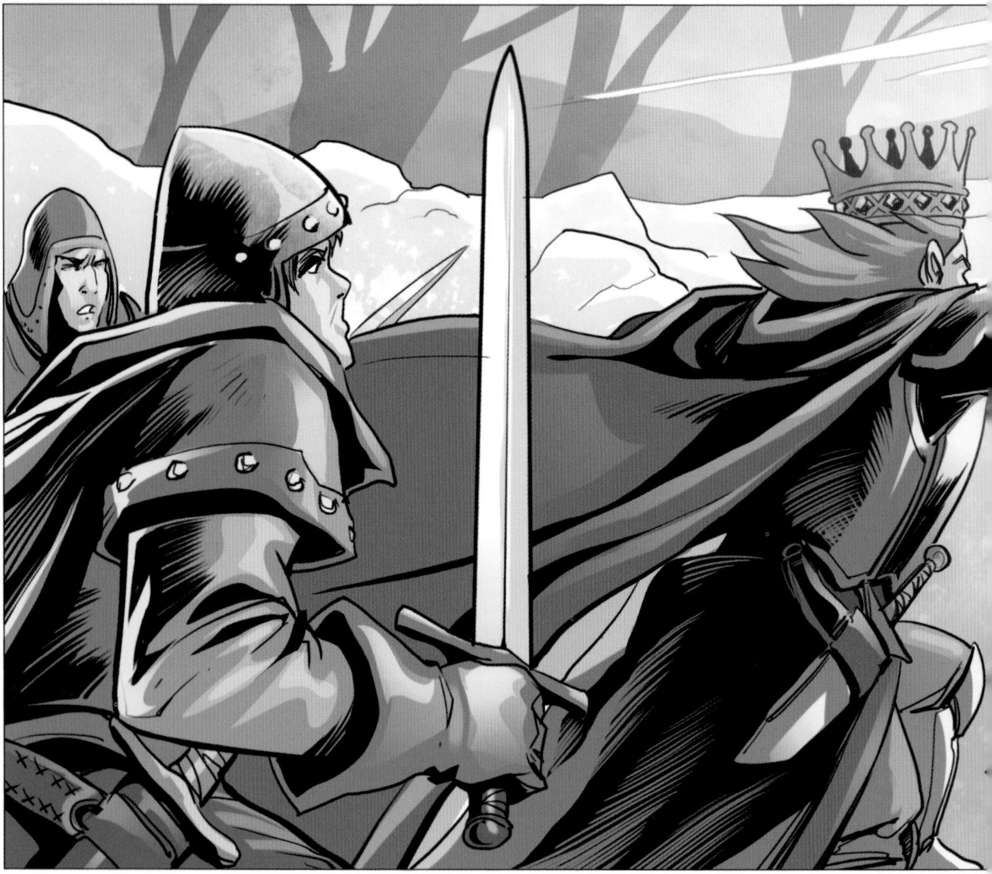

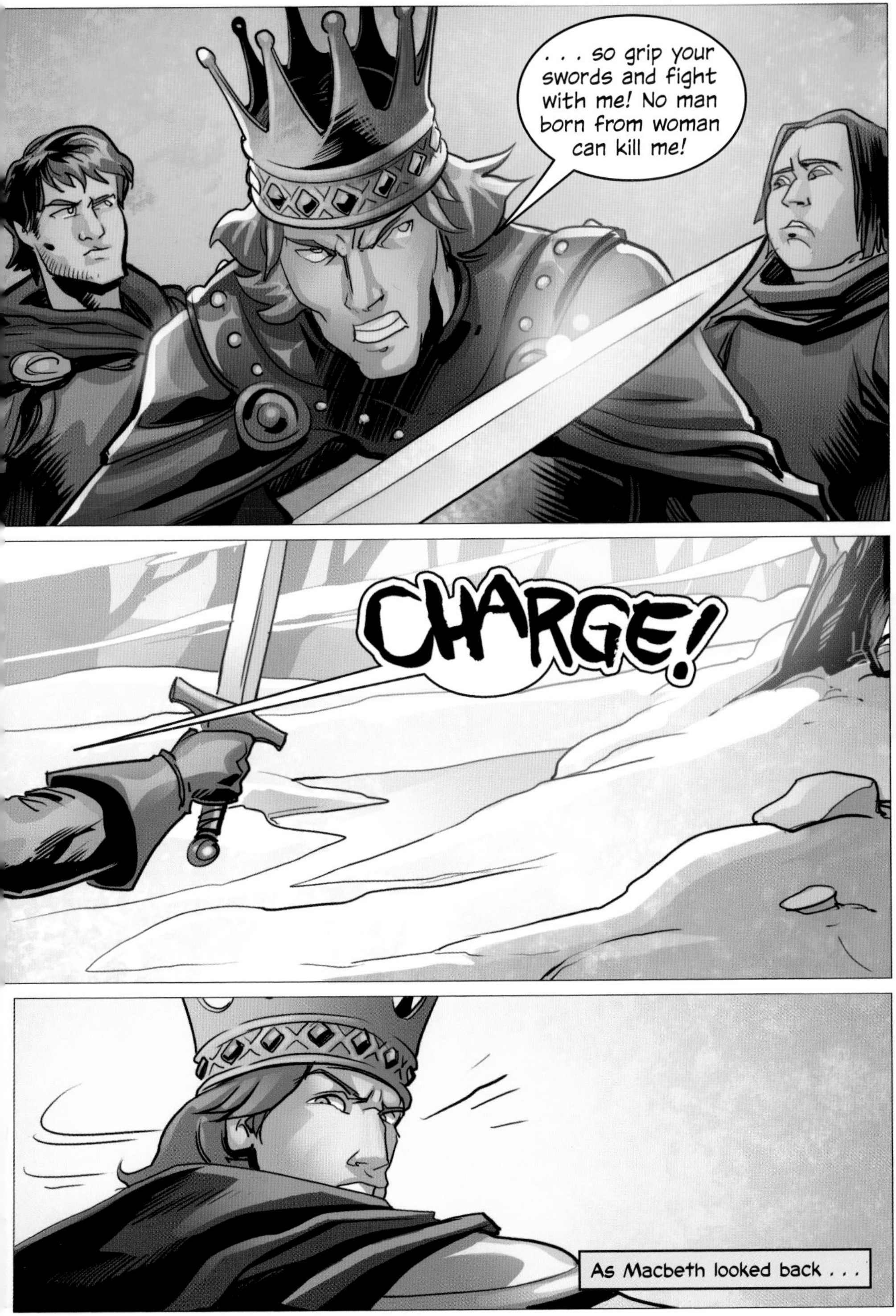
. . . so grip your swords and fight with me! No man born from woman can kill me!
CHARGE!
As Macbeth looked back . . .

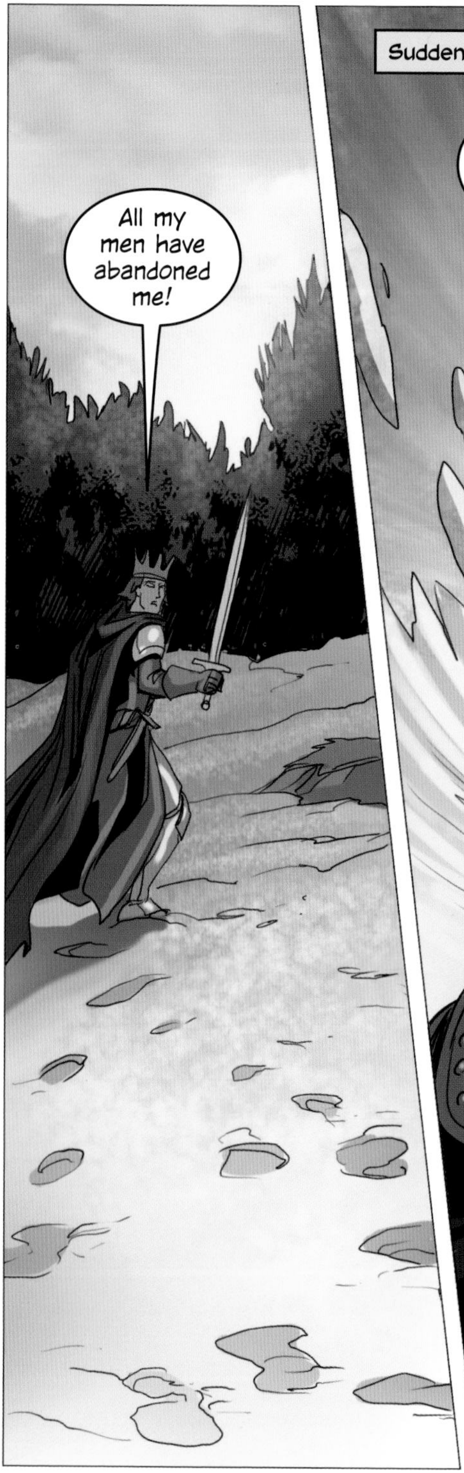
All my men have abandoned me!

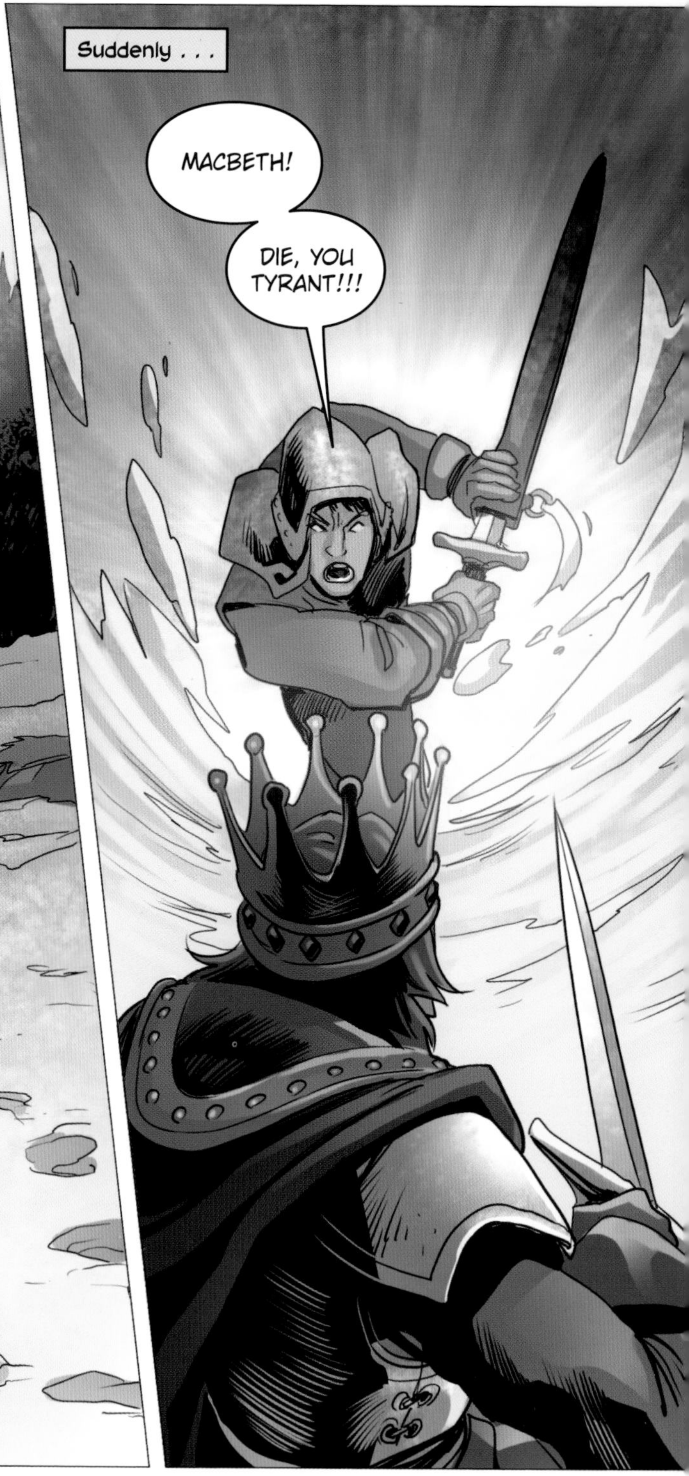
Suddenly . . .
MACBETH!
DIE, YOU TYRANT!!!

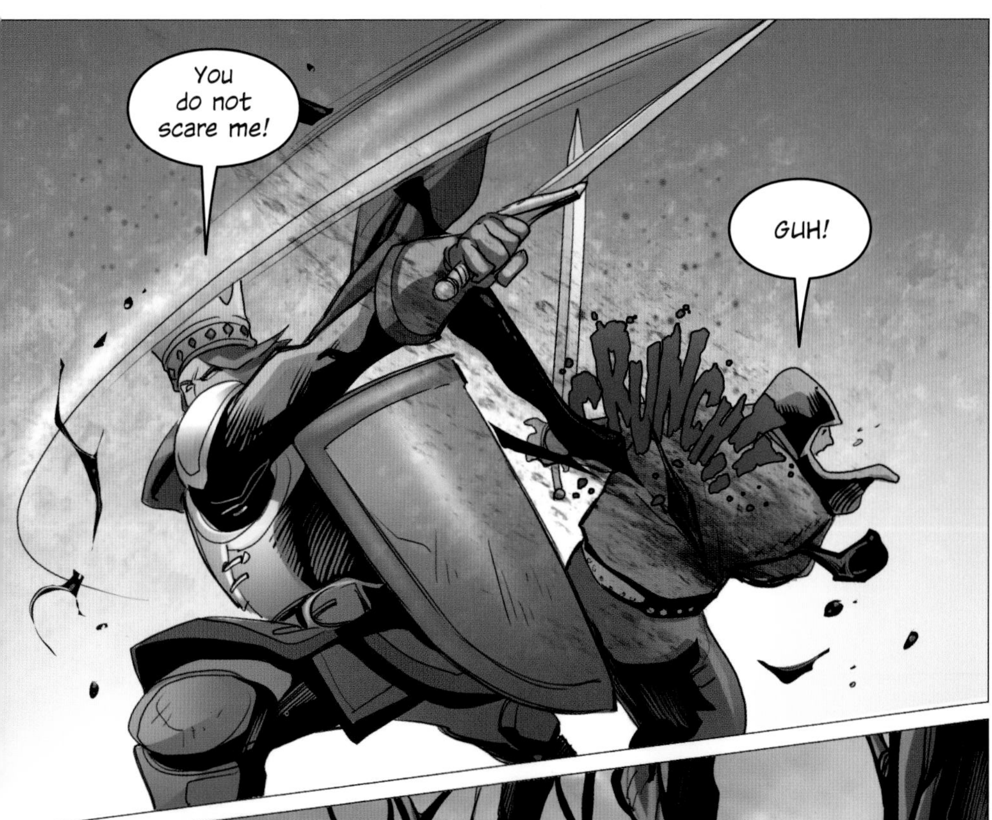
You do not scare me!
GUH!
CRUNCH!!

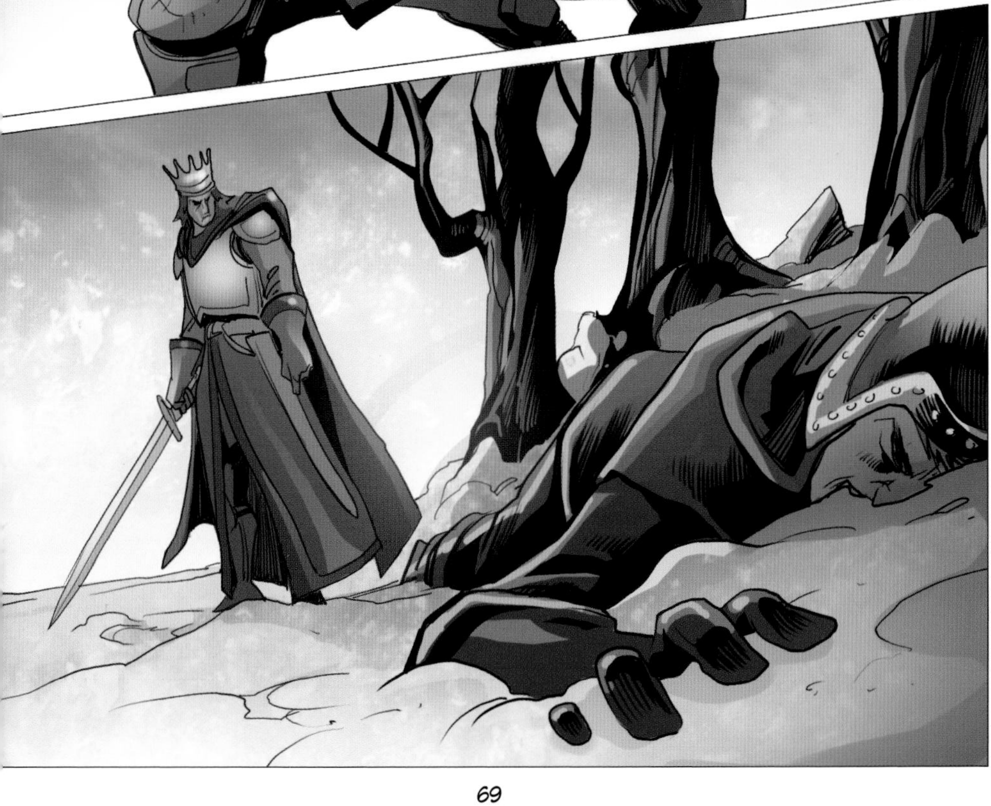

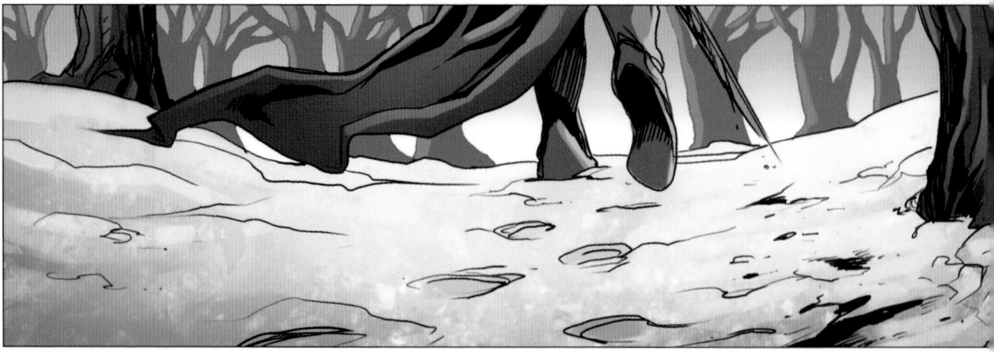

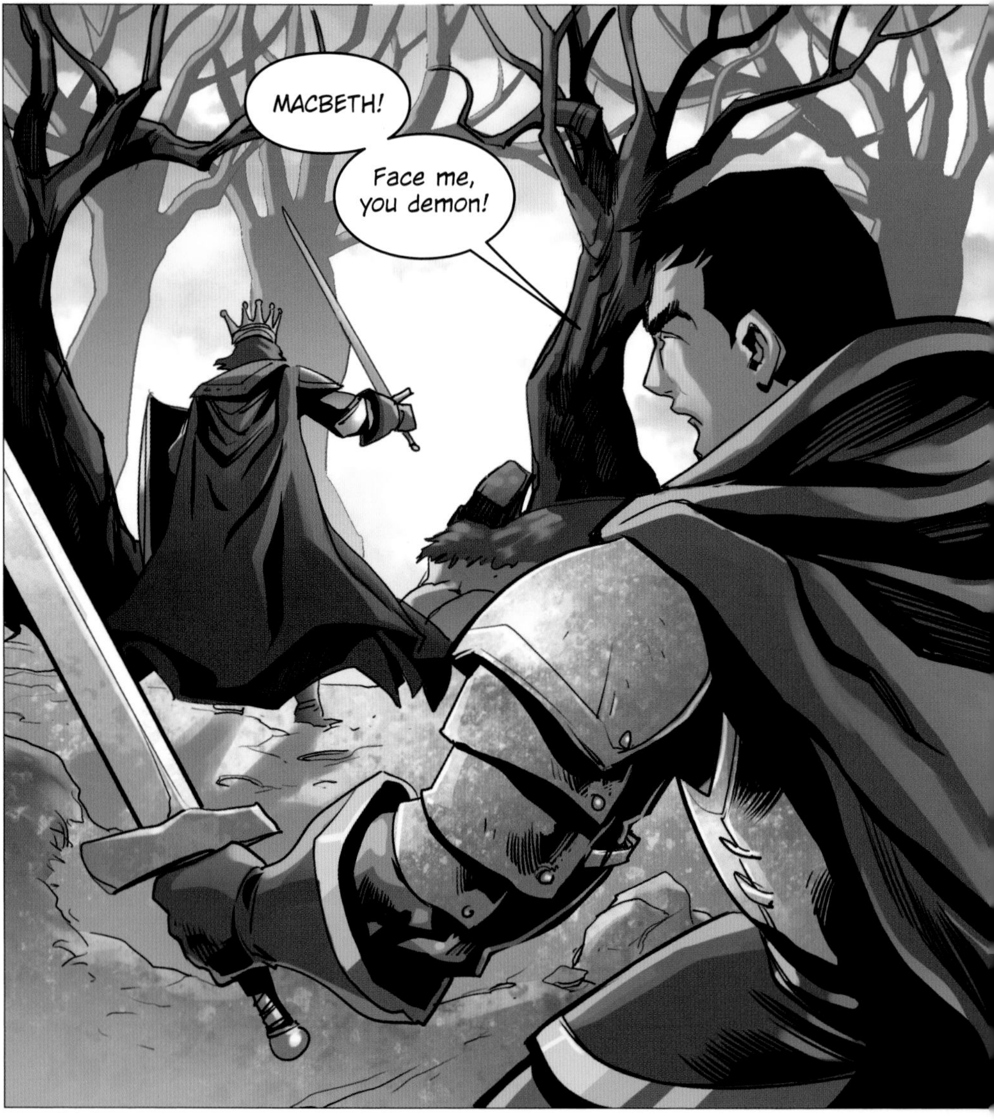

MACBETH!
Face me, you demon!

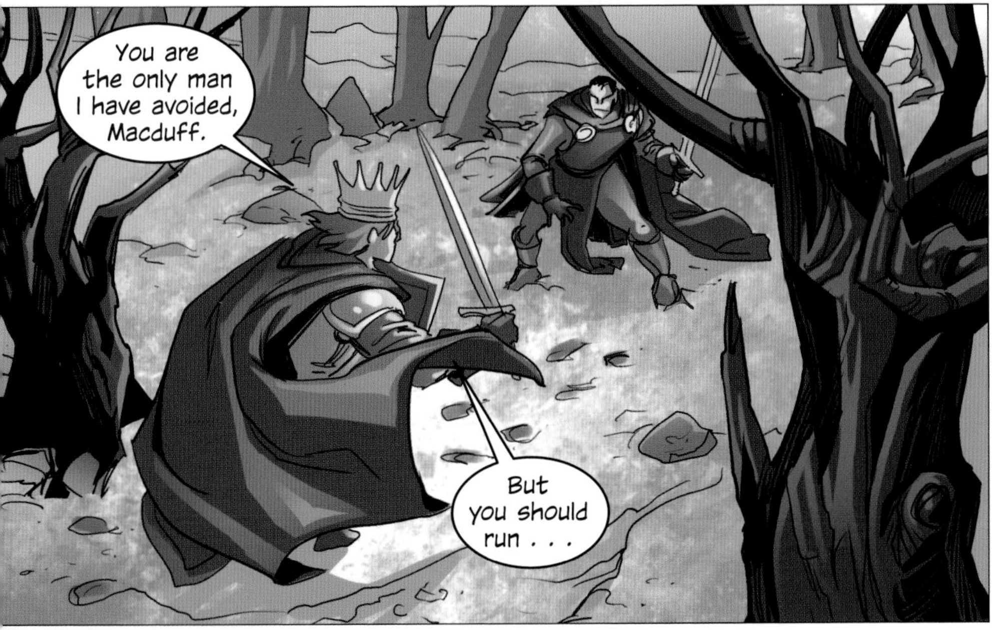
You are the only man I have avoided, Macduff.
But you should run . . .

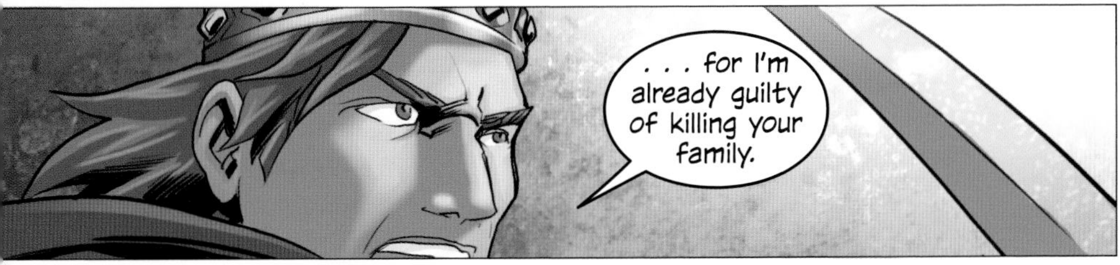
. . . for I'm already guilty of killing your family.

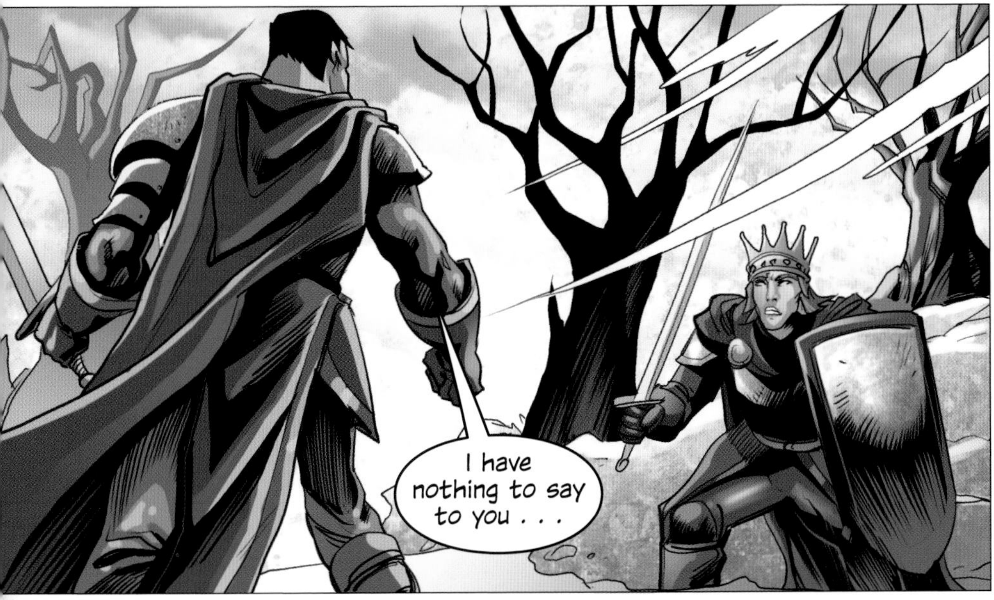
I have nothing to say to you . . .

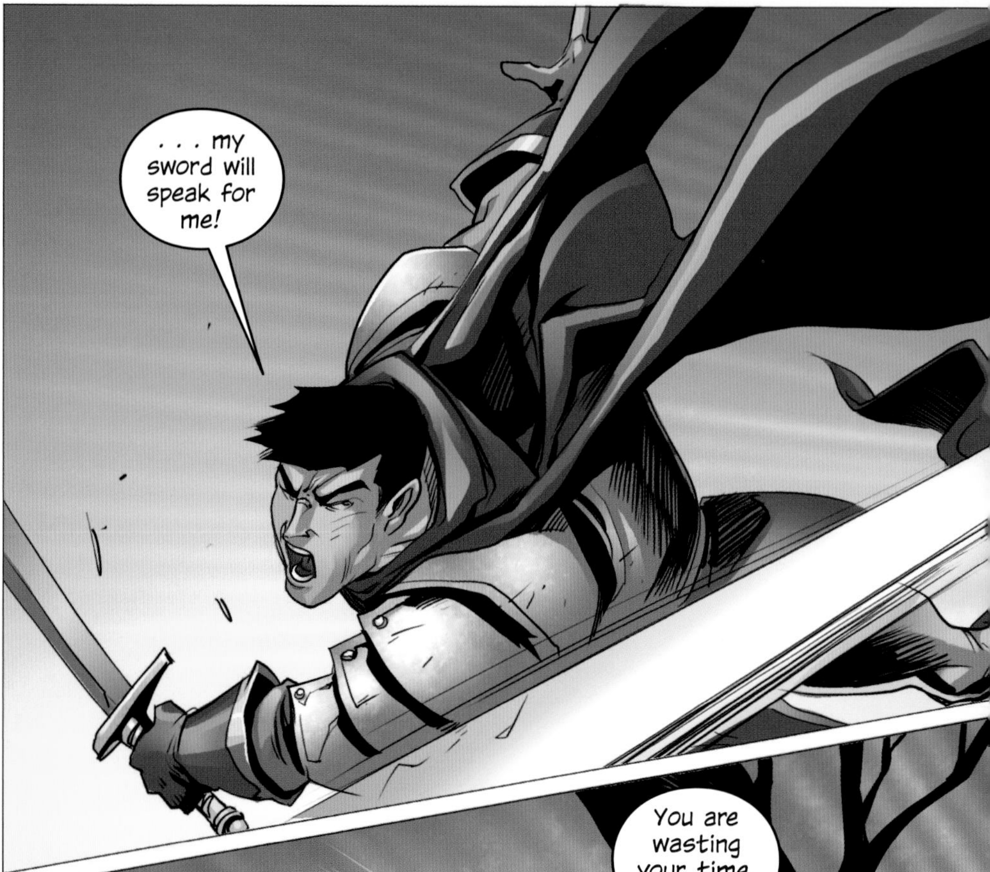
. . . my sword will speak for me!

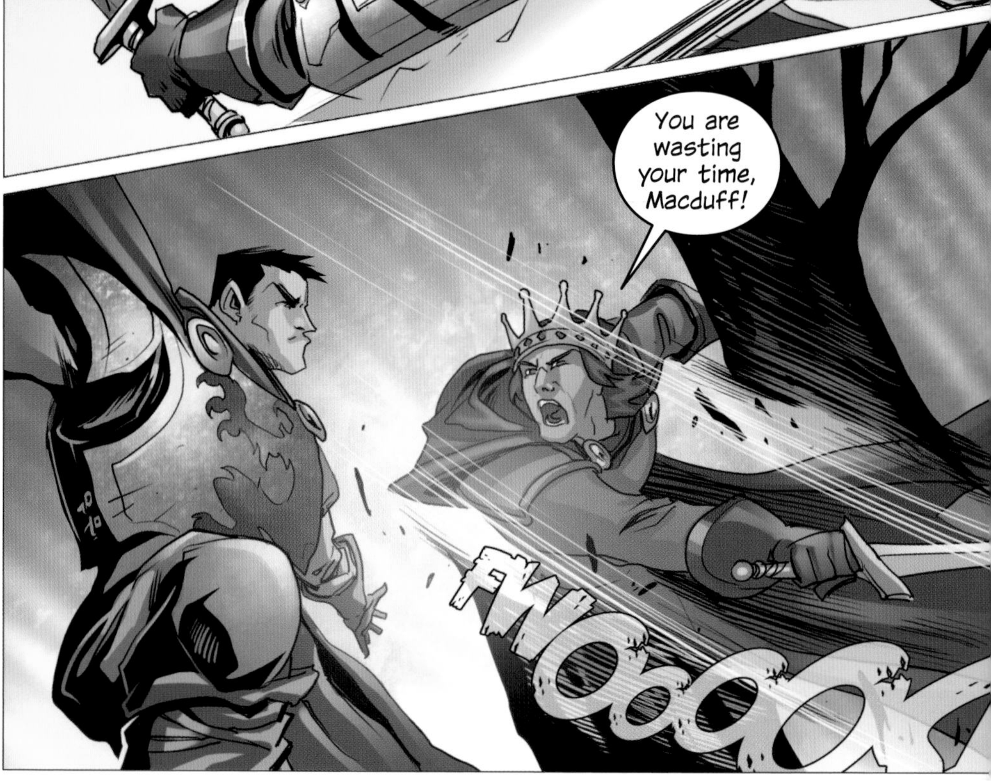
You are wasting your time, Macduff!
FWOOOO

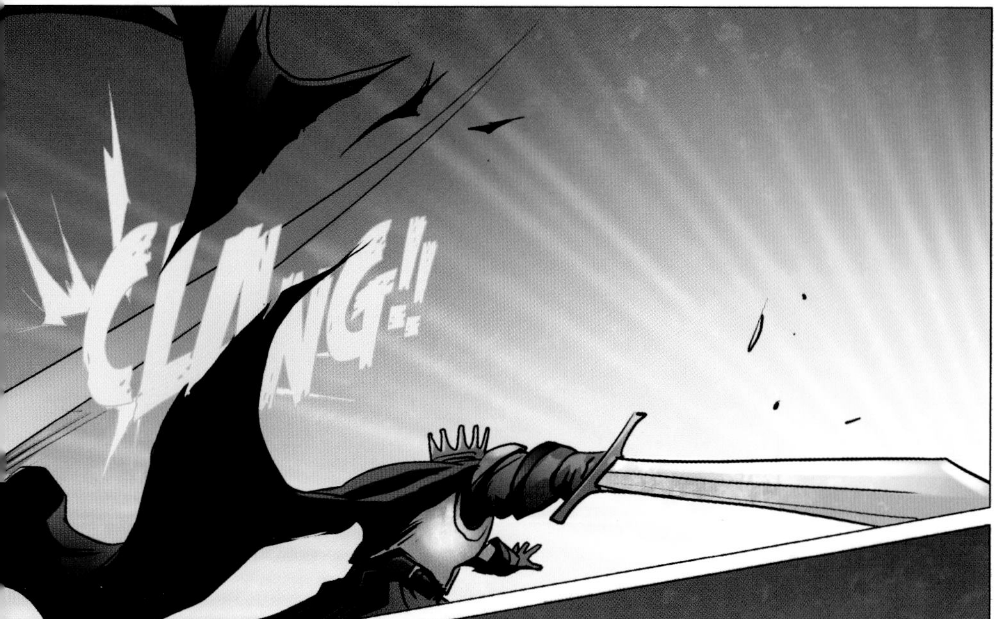
CLANG!!
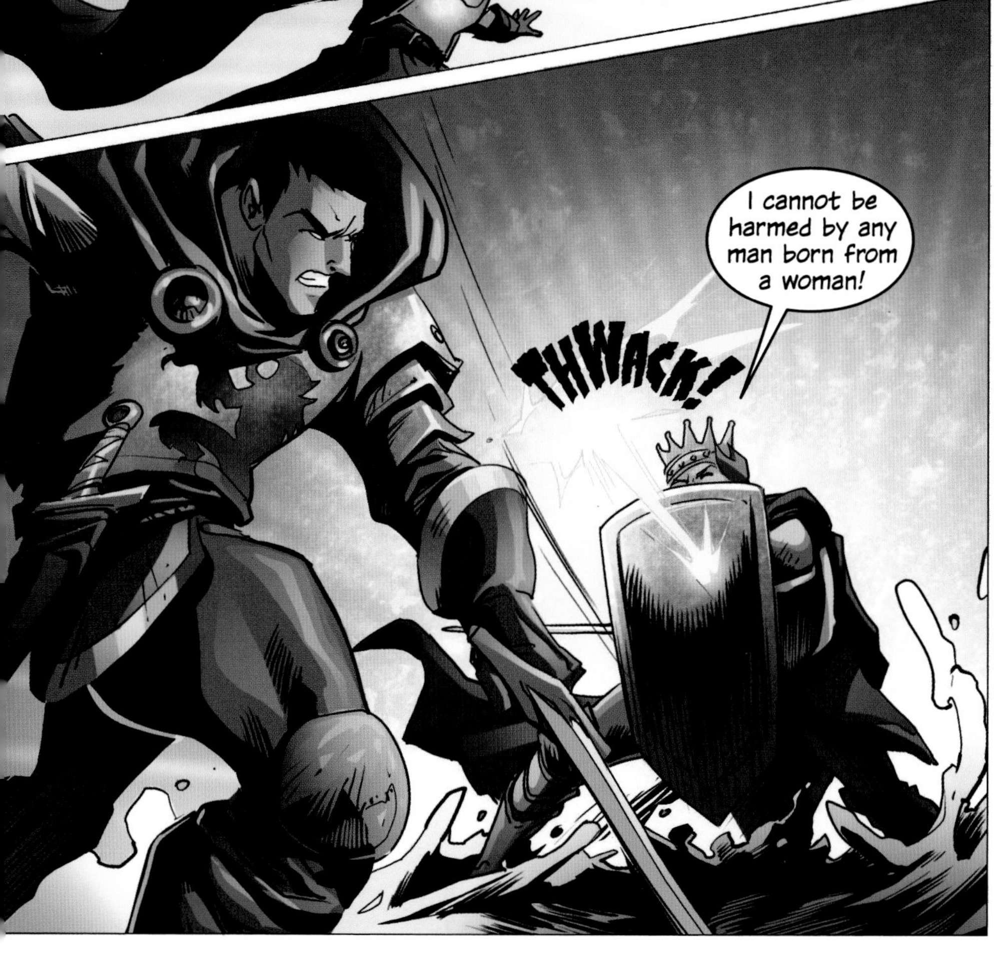
I cannot be harmed by any man born from a woman!
THWACK!

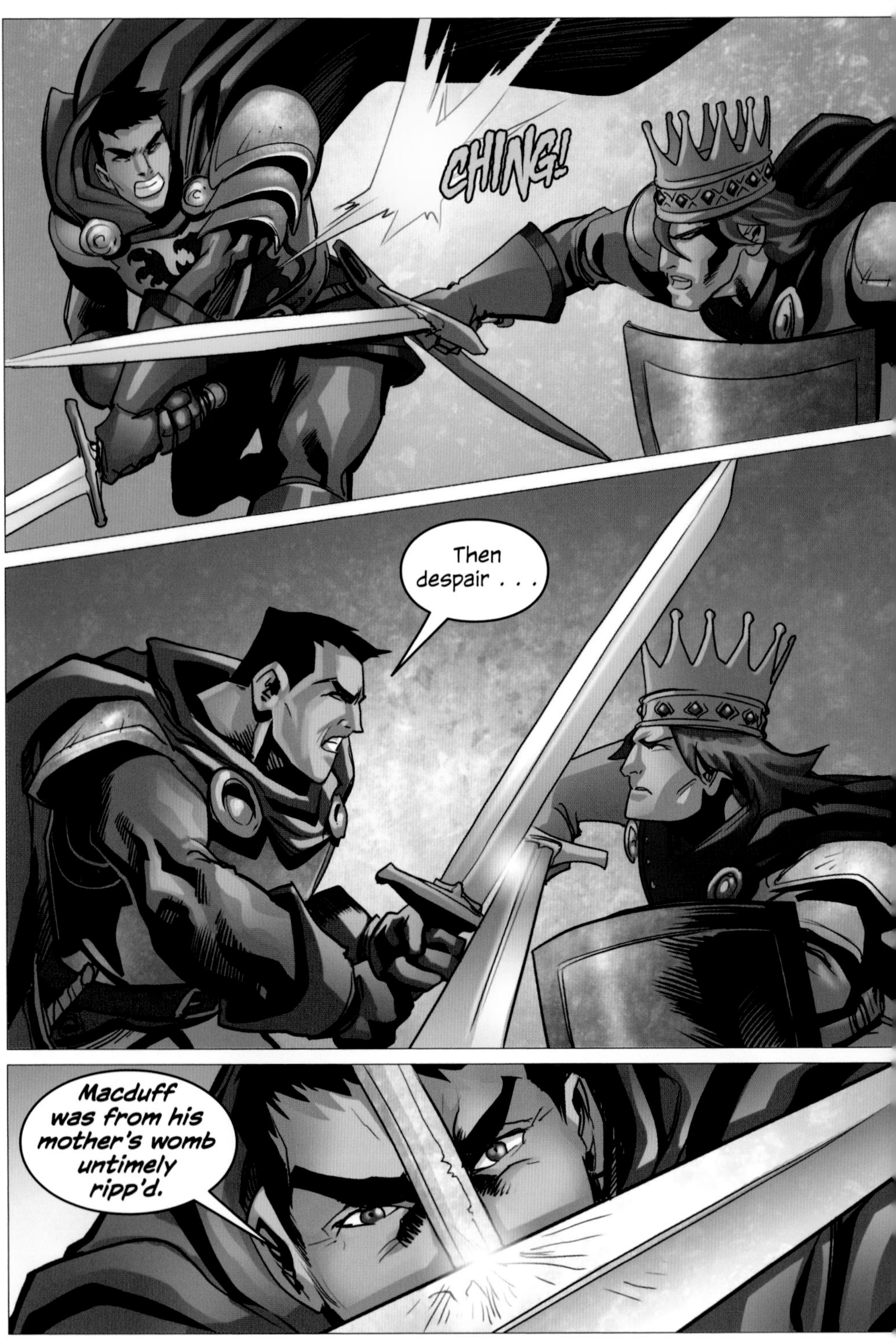
CHING!
Then despair . . .
Macduff was from his mother's womb untimely ripp'd.

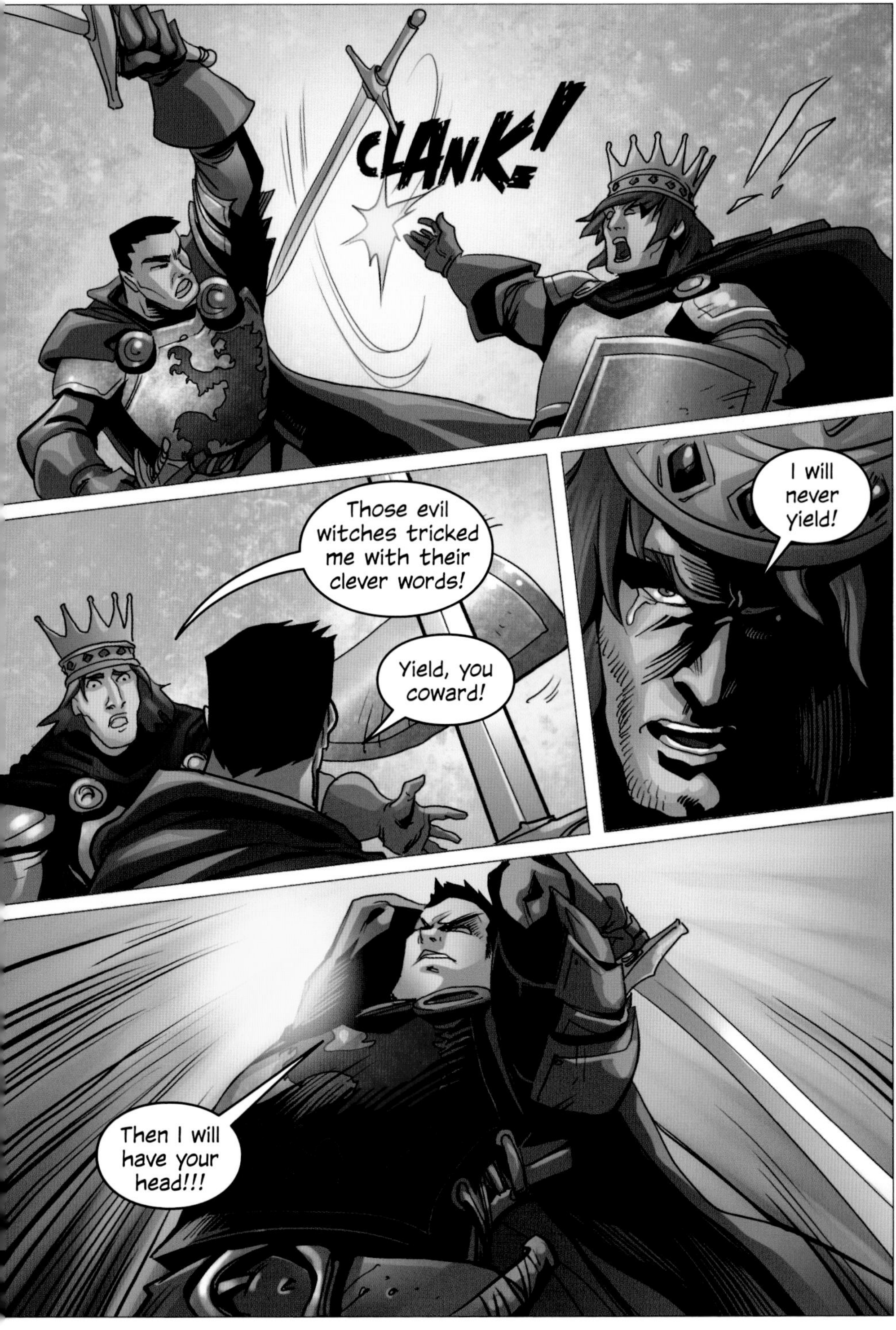
CLANK!
Those evil witches tricked me with their clever words!
Yield, you coward!
I will never yield!
Then I will have your head!!!

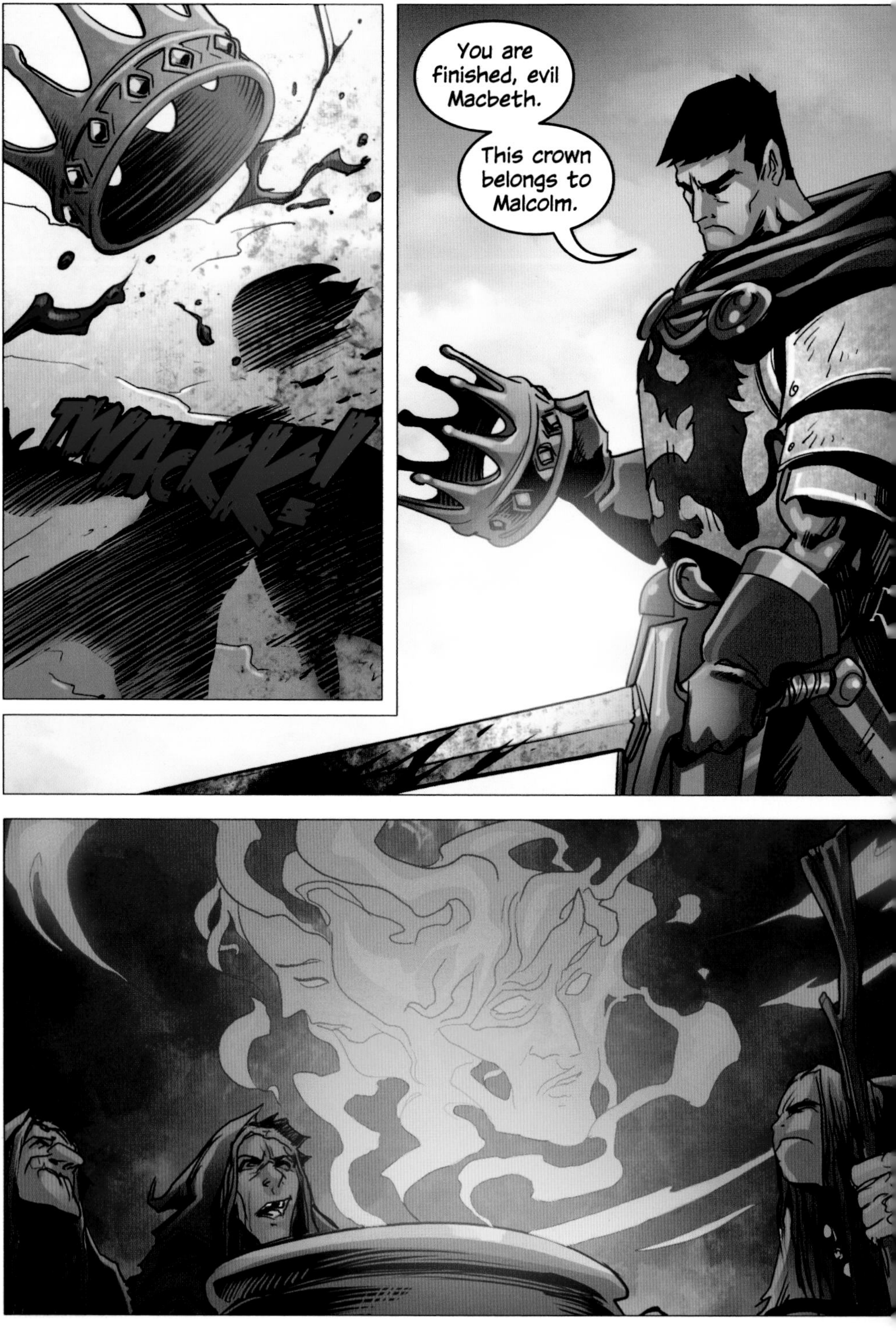
TWACKK!
You are finished, evil Macbeth.
This crown belongs to Malcolm.

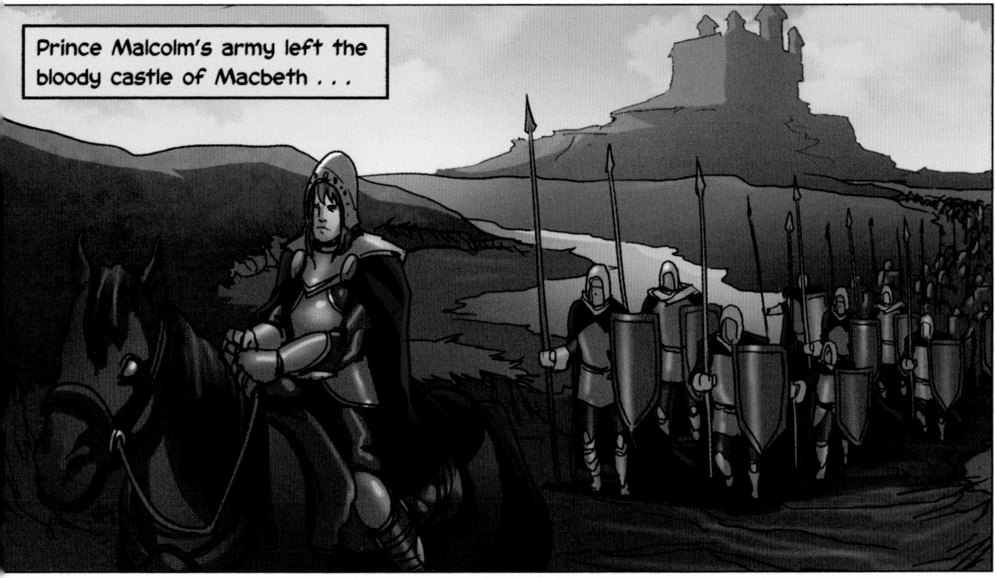
Prince Malcolm's army left the bloody castle of Macbeth . . .

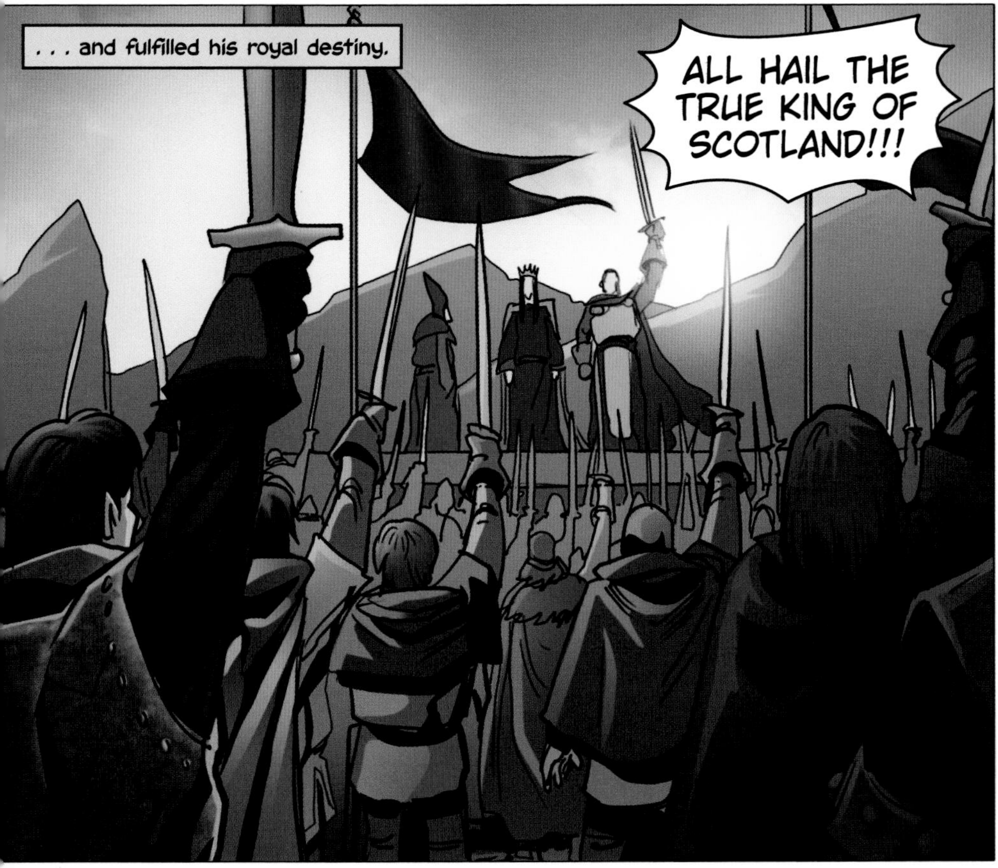
. . . and fulfilled his royal destiny.
ALL HAIL THE TRUE KING OF SCOTLAND!!!

ABOUT THE RETELLING AUTHOR

Since 1986, **Martin Powell** has been a freelance writer. He has written hundreds of stories, many of which have been published by Disney, Marvel, Tekno comic, Moonstone Books, and others. In 1989, Powell received an Eisner Award nomination for his graphic novel, *Scarlet in Gaslight*. This award is one of the highest comic book honors.

ABOUT THE ILLUSTRATOR

F. Daniel (Perez) was born in Monterrey, Mexico, in 1977. For more than a decade, he has worked as a colorist and an illustrator for comic book publishers such as Marvel, Image, and Dark Horse. He currently works for Protobunker Studio while also developing his first graphic novel.

ABOUT WILLIAM SHAKESPEARE

William Shakespeare's true date of birth is unknown, but it is celebrated on April 23rd, 1564. He was born in Stratford-upon-Avon, England. He was the third of eight children to his parents, John and Mary.

At age 18, William married a woman named Anne Hathaway on November 27th, 1582. He and Anne had three children together, including twins. After that point, Shakespeare's history is somewhat of a mystery. Not much is known about that period of his life, until 1592 when his plays first graced theater stages in London, England.

From 1594 onward, Shakespeare performed his plays with a stage company called the Lord Chamberlain's Men (later known as the King's Men). They soon became the top playing company in all of London, earning the favor of Queen Elizabeth and King James I along the way.

Shakespeare retired in 1613, and died at age 52 on April 23rd, 1616. He was buried at Holy Trinity Church in Stratford. The epitaph on his grave curses any person who disturbs it. Translated to modern English, part of it reads:

> *Blessed be the man that spares these stones,*
> *And cursed be he who moves my bones.*

Over a period of 25 years, Shakespeare wrote more than 40 works, including poems, plays, and prose. His plays have been performed all over the world, and in every major language.

THE HISTORY BEHIND THE PLAY

The Tragedy of Macbeth, commonly known as *Macbeth*, is believed to have been written by Shakespeare between the years 1603 and 1607. It was first published in the Folio of 1623, a collection of several of Shakespeare's plays.

Shakespeare used the name of King Macbeth of Scotland, a real king, for his main character. However, the real King Macbeth was a well-liked and noble king whose life had little in common with the play's version of the character.

In the play, the three witches tell Macbeth that anyone born from a woman cannot hurt him. Macduff, however, was born from a C-section — an alternative form of birth where a doctor surgically removes the baby from the mother's belly, instead of a natural birth. Macbeth thought the witches' words meant he was immortal, but really, the witches tricked him.

In the world of theater, the play *Macbeth* is considered to be cursed by many directors, actors, and stagehands! Some superstitious actors even refuse to say the name of the play, referring to it as "the Scottish play" instead.

Macbeth is one of Shakespeare's most popular and commonly peformed plays. It has been made into films, TV shows, operas, ballets — and graphic novels like this one.

SHAKESPEAREAN LANGUAGE

Shakespeare's writing is powerful and memorable — and sometimes difficult to understand. Many lines in his plays can be read in different ways or can have multiple meanings. Also, the English language was not standardized in Shakespeare's time, so the way he spelled words was not always the same as we spell them nowadays. However, Shakespeare still influences the way we write and speak today. Below are some of his more famous phrases that have become part of our language.

FAMOUS LINES FROM MACBETH

"But screw your courage to the sticking-place, and we'll not fail." (Act I, Scene VII)

SPEAKER: Lady Macbeth

MODERN INTERPRETATION: **If you keep your courage, then we will not fail.**

EXPLANATION: Macbeth says he is afraid that their plan will fail. His wife, Lady Macbeth, insists that they cannot fail as long as Macbeth stays strong and sticks with the plan.

"Infirm of purpose! Give me the daggers. The sleeping and the dead are but as pictures." (Act II, Scene II)

SPEAKER: Lady Macbeth

MODERN INTERPRETATION: **You coward! Give me the daggers. Dead and sleeping people, like pictures hanging on the wall, cannot hurt you.**

EXPLANATION: Macbeth refuses to bring the daggers back to the scene of the crime because he is afraid he'll wake someone who's sleeping, or meet the ghost of someone he just killed. Lady Macbeth explains that there is nothing to be afraid of and that she'll do it herself.

"Things without all remedy should be without regard. What's done is done." (Act III, Scene II)

SPEAKER: Lady Macbeth

MODERN INTERPRETATION: **If you can't fix something, you shouldn't worry about it. You cannot undo what is already done.**

EXPLANATION: Lady Macbeth tells her husband that they cannot change what has already happened, so Macbeth should stop worrying about what he can't change.

"By the pricking of my thumbs, something wicked this way comes." (Act IV, Scene I)

SPEAKER: A witch

MODERN INTERPRETATION: **The tingling in my thumbs tells me that something evil is coming this way.**

EXPLANATION: The witches cast their spell and conjure spirits to speak to Macbeth. The witch who speaks this line says she knows it is working because she feels a tingling sensation in her thumbs.

"Macduff was from his mother's womb untimely ripp'd."
(Act V, Scene VIII)

SPEAKER: Macduff

MODERN INTERPRETATION: **They cut me out of my mother's womb before she could give birth to me.**

EXPLANATION: According to the witches, Macbeth cannot be harmed by anyone born from a woman. Macduff, however, was technically not "woman born" because his mother had a C-section — an alternative form of birth where a doctor surgically removes the baby from the mother's belly, instead of a natural birth. The Witches' prophecy was a play on words; obviously, they were not to be trusted.

DISCUSSION QUESTIONS

1. Who is most to blame for Macbeth's death — the Witches, Lady Macbeth, or himself? Why?

2. Several characters in this book try to become king. What qualities must a good king have?

3. Which page of this comic book is your favorite? Why?

WRITING PROMPTS

1. Imagine that you're a king or queen. What kinds of laws would you make? How would you live? What would you do to protect your people? Write about your life as a ruler.

2. Shakespearean plays often have heroes and villains. Who do you think was the hero of this play? What about the villain? Explain your answers.

3. The three witches use magical spells. Create your own magic spell. What does it do? What would you use it for? Write about your spell. Then draw a picture of yourself casting it!

INTRODUCING ANOTHER SHAKESPEARE GRAPHIC NOVEL . . .

JULIUS CAESAR

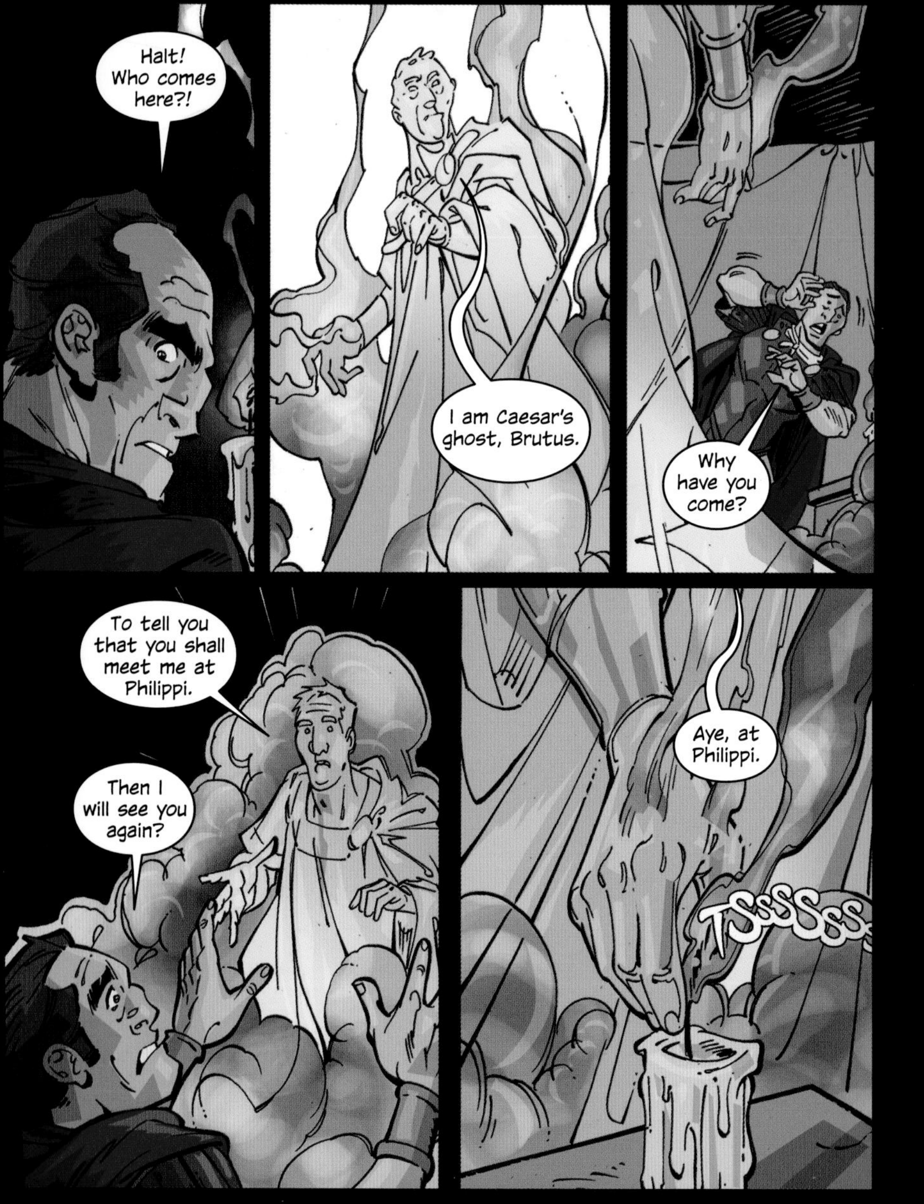
Halt! Who comes here?!
I am Caesar's ghost, Brutus.
Why have you come?
To tell you that you shall meet me at Philippi.
Then I will see you again?
Aye, at Philippi.
TSSSSSS

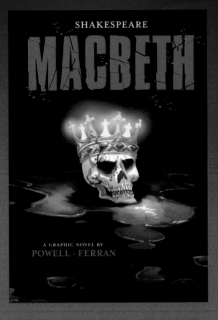
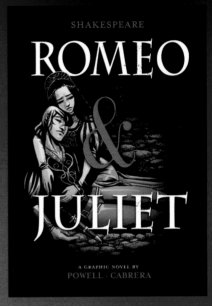
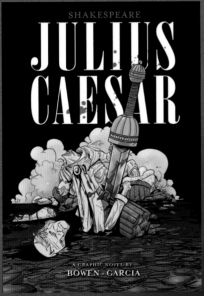
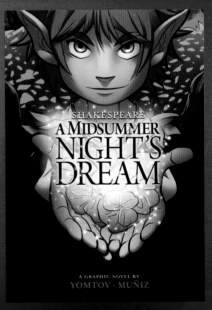

"ALL THE WORLD'S A STAGE."

— WILLIAM SHAKESPEARE